CABIN AT UNFORGIVEN

CABIN AT UNFORGIVEN

"Where tragedies and miracles collide…"

By: James D. Applegate

XULON PRESS

Xulon Press
2301 Lucien Way #415
Maitland, FL 32751
407.339.4217
www.xulonpress.com

Printed in the United States of America.

ISBN-13: 978-1-6312-9120-3

Dedication

I wouldn't quite say I'm thankful for my doubters, however, I will say they helped make this book better in many ways.

My parents, Bill and Betty Applegate, were always my strength from above. My father's last words to me were, "Finish that book, I want to read it...... see you when you get back from San Jose...". I think they may have both received an advance copy.

A very special thanks to my loving wife Kelly, who never doubted I could write this book. She did doubt I would stick with it, so for no other reason than that, I had to get "Cabin at Unforgiven" done.

.... And then there was my fourth grade teacher. She had little to do with this book being written, though she had everything to do with a turning point in my little messed up head. Thanks Mrs. Russell...

Table of Contents

CHAPTER 1: DEVILS SLIDE

TELEVISION STATIONS THROUGHOUT SOUTHERN Oregon and northern California were currently interrupting regularly scheduled programming with weather alerts. Big red bold banners flashed across the bottom of T.V. screens warning of the approaching Christmas day storm, by all accounts the biggest to hit the area in over forty-five years. One local meteorologist, Ben Blake, used a prop during a live broadcast to demonstrate the severity of the system dropping down from the Arctic. He shook a snow globe, then held in front of the camera, warning that this was the storm's potential. When anchorman Joe Hart had asked what viewers could expect on the summit, Ben Blake again shook the snow globe, this time vigorously, then turned it upside down.

His dramatic display came with a final statement to anyone thinking of driving on Christmas day, "DON'T ... just don't do it," he warned.

When Hart had asked about the summit, he was referring to the Siskiyou mountain range, a rugged divide between two states, California and Oregon. Most days, the jagged peaks of the Siskiyous remain hidden in a shroud of black or gray. Snow can fall three out of the four seasons, but don't rule out the occasional summer surprise.

Summer melting snow pack feeds streams that cascade over rock and silt before reaching the lush green landscape below. Here beneath pine canopy, wild animals roam freely. By night, they can be heard crackling across fallen debris covering the forest floor. In the winter months, only a few silently laid tracks can be spotted across the snowy landscape, left by the hungry, the predator and the prey.

At the valley floor the towering pines come to an abrupt final stance, giving way to the rich fertile lands of Rogue River Valley on the Oregon side. For generations, ranchers have lived here in the shadows of the Siskiyous. Miles and miles of mended fences are all that separate the wild animals from the domesticated. Out here, dirt roads and cattle far outnumber paved roads and people. Only a handful of small towns dot this lonely landscape, rising up out of a sea of patchwork grasses like little cement islands.

No matter which side of the Siskiyous you find yourself on, there is only one road that will take you up, over and down the other side. It's a narrow nightmare of a highway that has certainly earned its nickname of, 'Devil's Slide'. Once you enter the highest elevations, the inner lane scrapes the rocky edge on the mountain. The outer lane, however, has only a battered railing clinging to the edge, separating the road from the sheer cliffs.

Motorists are given one last exit before committing to the climb, a chance for food, a chance to get gas, and a chance to change their minds. For beyond this point, only a handful of rustic old hunting cabins lay hidden away in this rugged wilderness. Most of these crude structures are either abandoned or in the process of crumbling into the forest floor. Those that still stand, supply at best, a primitive shelter for hunters in the spring and summer months. Once the first snows fly, the human count drops to zero and the temperatures far below that.

Like a curly strand of black hair fallen across the Siskiyous, the road winds up one side and down the other. Driving by day, there is a view of the clear and present dangers on either side of the pavement. By night the road is desolate and dark with one's headlights occasionally catching the reflection of two glowing eyes of a wild animal peering out from the black forest.

Storms that pass over the Siskiyous can fool even the most seasoned forecasters. Locals will tell you that the only thing predictable about a storm running the highest ridges is that it will be predictably...unpredictable. In fact, during most winter storms, the gates at the base of either side of the mountain are locked shut. When this happens, not even the snow plows venture up into the unknown.

There are stories of those that slip by before the gates are locked. These drivers are referred to as the foolish...and or... the unfortunate. Sometimes drivers just blatantly disregard, while others are simply caught off guard. More often than not, these vehicles are found days later, disabled in a snow bank. Rescues, sadly, are not as common as body recoveries from these freezers on wheels.

Most fatalities on Devil's Slide are a result of driver's error. It was actually anchorman Joe Hart that gave the highway its iconic nickname. Early on in his career, he covered a story on the highway's deadliest accident. A lumber truck had lost control on black ice, sending it out of control into the opposing lane. There were seven people that did not come off the mountain alive. That night, Joe Hart made an emotional statement that grabbed everyone's attention. On air he reported, "Cascade

Highway runs right through God's country, but one mistake and a driver can find themselves on Devil's Slide."

CHAPTER 2: THE HEROES OF MORGANSVILLE

SOME STATES ARE SEPARATED by an invisible flat line, not California and Oregon. The Siskiyou Mountain range divides these two states with a border reaching an elevation of 7,500 feet. One of the little towns that lies nestled at the foot of the Siskiyous on the Oregon side is Morgansville, a sleepy little town that awakens once a year during a two day festival known as the "Beer Tip and Log Toss ". In these parts, Oregonians take great pride in the art of beer making, while taking even greater enjoyment in consuming that art. Like most Americans, they too enjoy their football, baseball and basketball. However, log tossing is one sporting event that seems synonymous with only the Northwest. Log tossers are to Oregon what Sumo Wrestlers are to Japan. Athletes of great size, with strength enough to lift a forty pound log, toss it as far as possible. This is quite similar to that of the track and field shot put event. Only here, they toss logs in between tipping beers of course.

For twenty seven years, Morgansville has had the distinct honor of hosting the Northwestern woman's heavyweight division of log tossing. This event brings beauty, brawn and beer to a makeshift stadium on the grounds of the Hurston Roberts lumber yard and funeral supply, an ideal location for readily available logs and yet an odd business combination, one might first think. According to Hurston Sr., his duel business makes perfect sense for capturing that customer for life. As he puts it, "I supply the lumber for one's first home and later the pine box for one's final home."

Eleven years running, the Bogner sisters have dominated the heavyweight division of women's log tossing. Bertha and Bess Bogner have achieved an athletic celebrity status in their sport, appearing in commercials throughout the northwest pitching everything from chainsaws to chewing tobacco. Together, the sisters have brought a greater awareness to the grunt-filled sport of log tossing.

There is also another reason that some visitors come to Morgansville. They come for an extended stay at a fortress-like stone building at the north end of town. Those that visit here enter through guarded gates. They are not really visitors as much as guests of the state, as this is the Tunnel Creek Prison. For the past twenty three months, one such guest has been an inmate by the name of Billy Canton Smith, better known by his nickname "BC ". He arrived here with a two year sentence for negligent manslaughter. Since both the incident and the conviction took place locally, the entire prison staff were familiar with his case. They all felt his sentence was far too harsh. In fact, only one person within the walls of the Tunnel Creek Prison felt his sentence was appropriate... and that was the convicted himself. None of this really mattered now. Tomorrow would be December the twenty fourth, and the last red "X" would be marked upon BC's calendar countdown to freedom.

Certainly there are those that live a life of crime, making a series of bad choices that bring them to a place like Tunnel Creek. BC's life was never like that. His was filled with unfortunate circumstances, beginning as early as his birth. The only time he shared with his mother was a time stamped on two certificates, his birth certificate and his mother's death certificate. As for BC's father, he abandoned his newborn, a decision that would forever change his life.

A father's desertion and a mother's passing while giving birth, were just the beginning of the unfortunate circumstances. BC's placement with adoptive parents began at age two and ended at age nine. For seven years, a secret was kept hidden by a child who only longed to be loved. It wasn't until an intuitive doctor asked the right questions that the abuse was brought to an end. This discovery also lead to BC's adoptive parents being arrested. Possibly the only thing more heart wrenching then the abuse were the screams of a nine-year old as his abusers were taken from him. They were, after all, the only family he ever knew.

Time can't change the past, it only allows for healing and clarity. Over the next few years BC came to understand the wrongs of his adopted parents, and thus, clarity. Eventually he was able to respect what the doctor had done for him. As for the healing part, that unfortunately was never handled professionally.

There is an unspoken truth that haunts the halls of most orphanages. The older the child, the less likely the chance for adoption. Nine-year old BC was far too young to be without a family. On the other hand, he was viewed as too old by adopting parents. His age prevented a second adoption from ever materializing. For the next nine years, BC would be bounced from facility to facility, celebrating his birthdays with kids he barely knew and adults that were simply paid to supervise. With his past haunting him and the present too painful, BC learned to escape into the future. After all, the future was whatever he wanted it to be, and so he dreamed ..... ambitious dreams, like becoming a doctor, just like the one who had helped him. As an adult, BC the man, set off to make his dreams a reality.

Medical degrees are not easily obtained by the homeless. At eighteen, with no family, he was just that, homeless, and penniless. It would have been easy to just give up the dream. Not for BC though, he put a plan into action. Joining the military seemed to be the only plausible option, serve his country while gaining a medical degree. After living most of his childhood within strict facilities, the young man instantly took to the disciplined structure of the military. For the first time in his life, he felt a sense of home. When eventually deployed to a foreign battle field, he performed his duties commendably.

All was going well until unfortunate circumstances once again entered in, this time during the heat of battle. In one brief moment of war, BC's heroic actions saved a great many lives, while at the same time putting an abrupt end to his military duty. Returning home severely wounded, he unknowingly entered into a new battle, one that involved too many doctors, prescribing too many medications. Before long, what was meant to help him actually became his new enemy. Prescription drugs altered his judgment, playing a detrimental part in an accident. Though his actions were unintentional, the outcome was deadly. Inside of a year, the soldier who fought for the freedom of all Americans found himself losing his own freedom.

From his conviction to his incarceration, BC never once placed blame on anyone other than himself. He also never made a plea for leniency. All he ever asked for was the opportunity to speak to the family of the deceased. This was promptly denied due to victim privacy laws. For BC, it was as if his apology, and any chance for forgiveness, were imprisoned right along with him at Tunnel Creek.

CHAPTER 3: HELLO KIDDO

TOMORROW WOULD BRING FORTH Christmas Eve, and for twenty-six-year old BC, his final day at Tunnel Creek. While packing up his belongings into a camouflage duffel bag, he reminisced about that December 24th two years earlier. He recalled how a cold chill came over his body as he faced the reality of his incarceration. Looking into his cell for the very first time, he observed a confining space with nothing warm or inviting about it, and why would there be, he was in prison after all.

Dressed in his assigned orange jump suit, BC stepped forward into his cell as directed by the guard that day. Behind him the jail door rolled across the tracks clicking three times as it locked shut. The sound reverberated through the corridors of the rock building. At about the same time the echo reached the furthest wall, his cell door again clicked three times, and rolled back open. He expected to see the same guard still standing there but that was not the case. What BC witnessed, reminded him of a magician's trick he once viewed on television. He recalled how a sheet was draped over a cage with a leopard inside. Seconds later the sheet was whisked away, the cat was gone and in its place was a young lady in a leopard print leotard. That is not what happened that day. When the cell door had reopened, there was no scantily dressed female, not even close. Instead, where the guard had been standing, an elderly grey haired lady now stood, leaning upon a pink cane.

"Hello Kiddo," she had greeted him that day.

At first BC could only muster up a bewildering stare as he tried to process in his mind what had just happened.

Still standing in the hallway, the elderly woman then asked, "So Billy, do I catch my death of cold out here, or do I come in?"

A half-hearted invite was given. As the two stood only feet apart, she promptly apologized for the slip up of calling him Billy.

"I know, I know, you wish to be called BC now," she corrected herself, " I still think if you wanted to sound more mature, William would have done the trick."

Her assumption for the name change had caught him totally off guard. Not because it bordered on rude, but because it was the reason he had changed his name, something he had never shared with anyone...

"Who are you?" he asked that day.

"Grandma C," she had replied.

"I mean what is your name?"

"Grandma C," she stated once again.

"Ok, so what does the 'C' stand for?"

"Just plain old 'C,' like in your name, only I have no 'B'... just a 'C'."

The gray-haired stranger then proceeded to sit on the edge of his bunk. He questioned her further, asking for the purpose of her visit. At first, she simply stated, "Because of you."

Immediately she realized her answer did not suffice the young man. So, she promptly expanded on her reply, telling him that her visit came about due to an answer he had left blank on his prison admission form. To be more precise, form 6A, his Weekly Visitors Request form allows for up to six people to be listed. He had listed no one. Because of this, Grandma C's boss made a special request, asking that she personally visit him once a week for the duration of his time at Tunnel Creek. This prompted a few more questions, like where did a ninety-year old lady work and who was her boss. At first, Grandma C acknowledged that both were understandably fair questions, then proceeded to give yet another evasive response.

"My boss and our organization must remain anonymous for now."

"So let me understand," BC countered back that day. "You want to visit me once a week?"

"That's the plan," she shot back.

"And... I get no name other than Grandma C, right?"

"Oh honey, you can drop the 'C' and just call me Grandma."

BC took a few minutes to process everything. Somehow his silence was taken to mean he agreed to the whole visitation idea. Next thing he knew, the gray-haired lady was planning out their next two years. By the end of their first visit, she even had BC writing a letter to the family of his victim. This was done in full knowledge it would never be sent. Her hope was that the process might prove therapeutic...that goal was achieved. Emotions of guilt and sorrow poured from his heart on to paper. What began as a single letter turned out to be a great many during his time at Tunnel Creek. On a shelf next to his bunk, a rubber banded bundle of letters grew by each week.

Over the next two years, Sunday visits with grandma, though always expected, still came with a bit of a surprise.

Normally, any individual making their way down the cement corridor could be heard long before reaching his cell. Somehow, grandma would just silently appear out of nowhere. With three taps of her pink cane upon the bars, the cell door would slide open and she would step in.

"Hello Kiddo," was her usual greeting.

Most visits began in prayer, something she had introduced to the young man. The rest of the hour was spent talking to one another. Grandma's boss had only one requirement. Their conversations were to focus solely on BC's past and, of course, his future. That didn't keep grandma, though, from sharing her wisdom and most importantly, her faith.

Since BC's only friends were still deployed, Grandma quickly became the center of his life over the next two years. Being bounced around as a child like he was, relationships just never happened. Ironically, his first real friendships were built during a war, and the closest thing to family he found while in prison.

From the very beginning, BC questioned Grandma on how she knew so much about his personal life. When he would ask, her answer was always the same, "I'm a grandma, we just know these things."

Maybe with a little investigative work, she could have learned about his childhood abandonment and abuse. As for his mental state upon entering Tunnel Creek, there was no way she could have known. BC had confided his feelings to no one. So how could she possibly have known of his contemplation over suicide. It was something he had considered, yet because of her entering into his life it was never acted upon.

Depression has an ugly way of burying the positive, while at the same time digging up everything negative from the past. If a person hasn't dealt with their issues, like BC, depression will use that to fuel the fires of doubt and self-pity. Sometimes it takes reaching the deepest darkest depths before a person will reach out for help. Fortunately for BC, help came to him and just in time. Over the following twenty-four months Grandma delicately performed what she called, "surgery of the soul." Grace, mixed with aged wisdom and a whole lot of prayer is how she operated. You might say, her surgery was a success.

During their visit yesterday, she had handed him a gift, a red leather-bound Bible. This would be their last visit together. There were tears as she left and he asked, "Will I ever see you again?"

The cell door clanked shut as she replied, "One day kiddo ... one day."

There was another person at Tunnel Creek that had been looking out for BC, Warden Ridge McCallister. He was a former military man himself, devout in the belief that once a Marine, always a Marine. Professionally, he viewed the young man as one of his prisoners, while at the same time respecting his battle field heroics. McCallister had made it his personal mission to find a temporary home for BC after serving out his time at Tunnel Creek.

Alone in his office, the warden was currently reclining back in his leather desk chair, his feet resting atop the cast iron coils of the wall furnace. In his hand, he held a newspaper article published the day that BC returned home from Afghanistan, an interviewed account portraying a single defining day in a military hero's life. Since the warden had read this article many times before, his eyes were not focused on the printed words this time, instead he envisioned that day as if he was there. Gazing out of his window at a misty rain, his mind was transported to a dusty battlefield in Afghanistan.

A tactical ground operation was the mission at hand that morning over two years ago. BC's unit was given clearance to transport a group of non-combative women and children to the safety of a mosque. Twenty-one displaced civilians were led through the backstreets of Kabul, flanked by BC and seven other soldiers. At one point, the designated route came to a long narrow alleyway. Perched on wall at the entrance of the passage between two buildings was a young Afghan boy. When he saw the soldiers he began to yell out to them.

"USA ...USA ...USA ".

Each time his voice projected a little louder with excitement. Cautiously both soldiers and civilians made their way into the entrance of the long vulnerable alley. Every window, door and inch of roof line were scanned by trained soldiers. One set of military eyes were drawn to the eyes of the perceived non-threat. As BC studied the young boy's facial expressions he noticed a discrepancy. Something about his demeanor didn't match up with the excitement in his tone. His brown eyes darted back and forth to the roof line directly above. His actions seemed more intentional then not. Based on these clues, BC directed his weapon towards the rooftop, at the same time he called for the others to retreat.

What followed was an eruption of gun fire raining down from above, met by the return fire from BC's M4. Before the lone sniper got off more than ten rounds he was neutralized. Most of his bullets only hit the wall resulting in powdery dust filling the air. Once it settled, the discovery was bitter sweet. There were those who could stand and shake themselves off ...and then...there was the little boy with the darting eyes, and the soldier who last looked into them. These two did not rise. Their bodies lay on the ground covered in debris, dampened by the flow of their own blood.

Injuries derived from shrapnel to his face, chest and hand would change BCs life forever, but thankfully he would live. For the bullet riddled body of the young Afghan boy, his life came to an end on that dusty backstreet of Kabul. That being said, had it not been for the vigilant actions of one soldier, the number of fatalities could have been much higher. BC often wondered if he was not the only hero that day. Were the darting brown eyes of the little boy an intentional clue to the deadly trap that lied ahead, or possibly the nervous reaction of an unwilling accomplice?

The Warden placed the article back into his desk drawer. Outside his window the rain had now switched to a soft falling snow. Plans for BC's life after Tunnel Creek now needed attention. A friend of the Warden's, Phil Meyer, owned the Cascade River Ranch on the California side of the Siskyous. There was always a need for an extra set of ranch hands. With nowhere else to go upon his release, BC gratefully accepted both the job and a place to live.

All that the warden had to do now was find someone willing to drive the young man over the Siskiyou's upon his release, someone who would be willing to do so on Christmas Eve. Only one person came to mind, one of his prison guards by the name of Landon Chase, a large man in both personality and sheer size. Tipping the scales at a consistent max employee weight limit of 275 pounds, his sheer size was intimidating to most prisoners. On the other hand, it also prevented him from sneaking up on devious behaviors. His massive thighs wrapped in polyester uniform pants, chafed like a couple of buzz saws. In a full-on run, it sounded almost like a swarm of bees on the approach. His tall stature came from his lineage, his girth, from all you can eat buffets. Everyone knew of his propensity to over eat, but few knew the secrets he swallowed down with each bite.

There was a reason the warden chose Landon, he was quite certain he had no plans for the holiday. His only relations that lived locally were his four ex-wives. It was safe to assume none of which had extended an invitation for the holidays. All the warden had to do now was entice him a little. That came in the form of a promised Christmas Eve steak dinner at the Cascade River ranch.

"Throw in a Christmas morning breakfast and you got yourself a driver," Landon replied.

"Done," the Warden shot back.

This left only one issue that was out of the Warden's control, the weather. Some stations were now even predicting it had the potential of becoming the biggest on record. The only thing that gave the warden any comfort was that the storm was not scheduled to hit until late Christmas eve.

Like many state-run facilities, the Tunnel Creek Prison had to follow a strict set of rules, even when they made absolutely no sense. For instance, the exact time stamped on a prisoner's release form must be followed right down to the second, without exception. The time stamped on BC's was 3:15 p.m.

Factoring in a two-hour drive had the men arriving just in time for dinner and a few hours before the storm was scheduled to hit. Of course, McCallister was well aware that storms in the high country often follow their own schedule.

CHAPTER 4: RETURN TO TRADITION

I
N A LAND OF suntans and convertibles, almost seven hundred miles from the Oregon border, the Kenwood family was preparing for a road trip up north. Parents, Dale and Kelly, had a yearly tradition of taking their family on a two day trek from Santa Monica, California to Pine Bluff, Oregon. Although certainly not recognized in any travel brochures as being a vacation destination, it happened to be where Kelly grew up and her parents still reside. Dale on the other hand, was California born and raised. According to him, the only thing the two states shared in common was that of a border.

Like years prior, their holiday tradition would begin the morning of December the 23rd. Breaking the trip up into two days, they would reach their final destination just in time for Christmas Eve dinner. Once there, three generations would commune together in one very small home. Grandchildren growing into teens, alongside grandparents growing out of touch, leaving a middle generation to grow weary from both. Grandma's regimented schedule of festivities was best enjoyed in small doses. When the family could, they would escape from the excitement of board games and head out to nearby Mt. Bachelor for some skiing.

Excluding last Christmas, the Kenwood's had made the drive north fourteen years in a row. Each time they entered into the grandparent's little corner of the world they found themselves inevitably stepping back in time. Bill and Betty Applegate stopped advancing with technology about the time the microwave was introduced. Even a simplistic essential kitchen appliance such as this proved to be too advanced for the tech challenged couple. After using it only one time, Bill tossed out the dangerous device with a spam-roast still smoldering within. He immediately called his daughter Kelly, the one who had given them the microwave as a gift. With the phone receiver in one hand and a fire extinguisher in the other, he shouted in anger while the home's smoke alarm blared in the background. She tried her best to explain that the cast iron pot was the reason for the fire. Her explanation was in futility. As sirens could be heard on the approach, Bill yelled into the receiver, "What good is an oven you can't put a pot in?"

The fact that Bill and Betty raised only one child was probably for the best. As a mother now herself, Kelly observed how her parents transitioned from a strict regimented reign of parenthood into Disneyland grandparents. Growing up, she was never allowed to sit in her father's naugahyde recliner, and as for her mother's prized white satin sofa, it was for adults only. If Kelly so much as skipped across the shag carpet, her father would yell, "this is not a playground, go outside." Oh how things had changed. In recent years, she witnessed her father launching her children one by one from his recliner, shooting them across the room feet first into the white satin sofa. Before each was launched, he called out, "Step on up," like some demented denture wearing circus carny. Kelly was stunned by the change, not to mention, just a little jealous.

Despite all this, visits with the grandparents were a treasured time for the entire family. Each year came with a spattering of new memories wrapped up in a whole lot of past predictability. Bill and Betty lived within a regimented routine that rarely rambled off course. From the very moment the family would arrive, the past would begin repeating itself. Regardless of whether they were early or on time, grandpa would inevitably be standing on the front porch holding his pocket watch shaking his head in the winter cold.

"You're late!" he would yell out.

Most times, he would then hurriedly hand out a few hugs while making his way to the driver's door. Before his liberal son-in-law could even exit the vehicle, Bill would start in with one of his unsolicited far right political rants. Views so far right that normal Republican views seemed left. These politically charged rants were fueled by a single strong desire. Bill, in his own loving way, felt he was rescuing his daughter and son-in-law from the misguided clutches of the liberals. Debating with Bill on anything political was no longer an option, a lesson learned after the all night great debate of Christmas 2014. After that, Kelly and Dale implemented a technique perfected by their very own children. Pretend to listen, nod occasionally, and then go on doing, or in this case believing, as you were.

As for Grandma, she usually made her first appearance from inside the front window, her body framed by an outline of vintage Christmas lights. Some of the mega-size bulbs flickered in and out, while others were broken or just missing all together. About four years back, Dale noticed that Bill's solution to duct-tape over the empty sockets had then outnumbered the actual lit bulbs two-to-one. When he offered to replace the strand with a new one, his father-in-law replied, "Your mother-in-law is not as bright as she use to be... do you suggest I replace her with something new as well?"

The truth be told, Betty never shined more than when she was surrounded by her grandchildren. In the excitement to see them, the floodgates of joyous tears would always flow down her powdered red cheeks. As each family member entered the home, they would receive one of grandma's signature tear soaked hug–kiss combinations. At least one person would also receive the red rouge mark of Betty on their clothing, more often than not, the last in the door, Dale.

Then like a shot out of a cannon, Grandma would usually race back to her kitchen to attend to last minute preparations. The aroma of the Christmas Eve feast intertwined with Bill's smoldering cigar was an unusual combination to say the least. Adjusting from the bitter cold outside to the soothing warmth within came quickly. Between the wall heaters, the space heaters and the wood burning stove, it didn't take long for soothing to become sweltering. Cloth napkins at the formal Christmas Eve dinner table often doubled as sweat dabbers for those under eighty years of age.

If this year was to play out like years past, there would be no relaxing after Christmas Eve dinner. Bill and Betty had a regular routine of disappearing after dessert, only to reappear ten minutes later in their Sunday best. Grandpa would use part of this time to warm up the old Cadillac station wagon for the short drive to the Pine Bluff Baptist Church. It should be noted, there were a couple of interesting facts about Grandpa's car. One, he purchased it back in 2001, used, or in this case, retired from service. Second, the car was sold to him as a limited production station wagon with unique features, such as a rear loading door and a six foot pull out tailgate, perfect for Sunday picnics. The morbid truth though, was this bright red Cadillac station wagon had once been painted black. It was only after a second row seat had been added that the former hearse took on a new life, so to speak, as grandpa's family station wagon. Every year, the Kenwoods would pile in through the rear door for the slow ride down Main Street.

Along the way, Betty usually tended to her husband's last minute grooming needs. This might include brushing away cigar ash from his black tweed coat or even plucking an ear hair if needed. With two hands firmly on the wheel, none of this ever seemed to interfere with his driving. He always maintained a careful speed down Main Street right in pace with last minute Christmas shoppers...those on foot that is. For those in their cars, they were forced to follow at Grandpa's safe speed of 5 mph. By the time the slow turn into the church's parking lot was made, there usually were one or two horn honks of anger.

The year before last, one man yelled out, "where's the funeral?" somewhat ironic seeing as to the Cadillac's past history. That same year, the horn honking had caught the attention of church goers waiting in line to greet the pastor at the front door. Oblivious to the crowd of onlookers, Grandpa pulled right on up to the entrance curb. What startled the pastor, and even scared a few of the elderly in line, was the loud scraping sound of the weighted down rear bumper as it tore across a speed bump. As if unaware of anything embarrassing, Grandpa exited the former hearse right there smack dab in front of a stunned crowd. He cordially escorted his wife out of the car, shook hands with the pastor, and then returned to his driver's seat. The rest of the passengers behind the privacy window opted to exit once the car was parked.

Memories like this, and many more, came from a tradition that abruptly ended two years earlier. Christmas before last, tragedy struck the Kenwood family. Bobby, their youngest child who had been fighting cancer most of his young life, passed away while in Oregon that year. Doctors had done everything they could for him. His medications were just no longer working. That didn't stop Bobby from wanting to see his grandparents that year. He had insisted they make the trip. In an odd twist of fate, his death was not a result of cancer. Bobby was struck down by a snowmobile while he and his father were playing at a snow park.

Over the last twenty four months, Kelly along with the two youngest daughters, thirteen-year-old Amber and fifteen-year-old Makayla, had attended a survivor's class together. They learned how to mourn Bobby's passing less, by celebrating his life more. As for Dale and the eldest daughter, seventeen-year-old Meagan, they were behind in the healing process.

Despite the past, the family was in agreement to return to tradition this Christmas. No one was more excited about this than Grandma Applegate. Throughout the year Grandpa had randomly called out to his wife, "Hey my little Pine Nut, how many days until the grandkids arrive?" Without hesitation, she replied each time with the exact number of days. Last year's canceled visit had been very hard on the grandparents. Somehow, Bill found a way to blame his son-in-law, just as he blamed him for his daughter never returning home after college. The fact that she chose a school in sunny California to begin with had nothing to do with Dale and everything to do with Oregon. Growing up in the shadow of the Siskiyou Mountains, there were really only two seasons, the Gore-Tex season and Parka season. Being stuck inside more often than not, Kelly referred to her home state of Oregon as "Bored-again."

After careful consideration, the Applegate's only child picked a Southern California college to attend. UCLA seemed to be that perfect match for both her educational and climate needs. Kelly also had a secret desire of maybe meeting a California boy, like the suntanned surfer on the schools promotional brochure sent out to recruit students from the pale skinned states. Jumping ahead six years, Kelly received a doctoral degree in Biochemistry about the same time she received an engagement ring from a young doctor. The two met via a blind date orchestrated by a mutual friend, Michelle. She enticed Kelly by telling her that Dale was a surfer and, oh by the way, he drove a red convertible. "I think it's a Corvette," Michelle added.

Unlike a great many blind dates, this story had Dale falling for Kelly every bit as hard as she fell for him, inseparable from that first date on. Their friend, Michelle, had mastered the match making process except for one slight misstatement. Dale did not drive a convertible Chevy Corvette. He drove a convertible Chevy Corvair. For Kelly, it didn't really matter. By the time she was throwing her graduation cap into the air, wedding plans were being made.

Twenty years and four kids later, the Kenwoods now own and run a multi-million dollar biotech company in the Los Angeles basin. Their 14,000 square foot home within a gated community commands an unobstructed view of the Pacific Ocean. Almost anything the family could want, they purchase, and if something better comes along, they purchase that too. Of course, this is in sharp contrast to how Kelly once lived, and how her parents currently live. In Grandpa's frugal mind, "If it ain't broke, why replace it?" However, if something did break, out came the single greatest invention of all time according to him...the fix-all... duct tape. He once used it to fix a hole in his fishing canoe, the very same one that now sits at the bottom of Crow Canyon Lake.

Dale and Kelly have tried to bring her parents into the modern age with absolutely no luck. Even the grandkids attempted several years back, when they insisted they give the grandparents a Christmas gift of a cell phone. Grandpa would have nothing to do with this device, claiming their land line was more than adequate.

After handing the Christmas gift back that morning, he tried his very best to show his grandchildren why they had no need for a mobile phone. With all four in tow, he grabbed the lime green rotary phone off the kitchen wall. Since it was the only phone in the house, it had an expandable cord. Holding the receiver up to his ear as if he was on an actual call, he asked that they follow him through the dining room.

With the partially duct taped cord draped over his shoulder he headed straight for his recliner. Along the way his spectators found themselves ducking and swaying to avoid the air born cord. At one point it struck a lamp. This in no way deterred Grandpa from further making his defense against the need for a mobile cell phone. Heading down the hallway towards the bathroom, he displayed how it reached all the way to his second favorite seat in the house. Feeling as though he had proved his point, he made his way back towards the kitchen. Again the cord wildly whipped about flipping a filled ashtray onto the shag carpet. Clean up of the cigar butts was quickly aborted by Betty. She moved on to the dining room, taking a protective stance over her fine china. Bill swung the cord up and over her grey head of hair, missing the stemware, but striking the table top nativity scene instead. This sent the Baby Jesus airborne out of the manger and Betty diving in for the Hail Mary save. The cord was now wrapped around the star of Bethlehem that clung to the top of the manger by only a weathered old strip of duct tape. Bill was now standing in the kitchen where he made one last yank. Upon doing so, the elasticity in the telephone cord worked much like that of a sling shot, shooting the star of Bethlehem through the air. Unfortunately the wooden projectile hit a freshly poured cup of coffee in Dale's hand. His cashmere sweater already stained by Betty's red rouge was now splattered in coffee.

"See, I don't need a cell phone!" Grandpa proclaimed that day.

Dale sarcastically replied, "Well you certainly convinced me."

Oddly, moments like this, with the separation of time, became some of the most treasured memories. The youngest daughter, Amber, could not wait to get back to the memory making. Somehow in a family of blue eyed blondes, a freckled faced red head came to be. On either side of the family tree, there was not even a third cousin once removed with red hair. Being the youngest of the girls, she had to learn to become assertive. After learning that, she then mastered the art of antagonism...and why not, she had two great teachers.

One of those teachers was her sister Makayla. A snow white blond with eyes as blue as a Montana Sky. Frequent compliments from friends and strangers alike on how beautiful she was, had her sisters often wanting to pop her inflated ego. It certainly didn't help that the family's home was overrun with her beauty pageant trophies, proud achievements for Makayla and a source of jealousy for the sisters. Since the passing of her little brother, she seemed to hide out more and more in her own little fairytale world.

If there was one sibling that struggled with Bobby's death more than the others, that would be Meagan. When she first learned about her little brother's cancer she never once cried. She instead made him the most important thing in her life. Every free moment she had, she spent with Bobby, even going as far as to sleep on the floor next to his bed most nights. She would whisper happy little stories until he would fall asleep. Quite often a bad reaction from chemo would awaken them both. Meagan was there to escort her little brother to the bathroom, never once leaving him to be sick on his own. Kneeling next to him she would rub his back until he was well enough to return to bed. It was during one of these late night episodes that Meagan had made a promise to Bobby, a promise she was not able to keep. As Bobby became sicker and sicker, she slipped further and further away. Her unfulfilled promise had her isolating from her family, including her little brother.

After Bobby's passing, Meagan's isolation continued. An eating disorder also joined forces against the teen's well-being. Attempts were made by the parents on multiple medical fronts to help their daughter. Their tearful concerns were often shared from the opposing side of a slammed bedroom door. Good parents never give up, and yet, sometimes they just don't know what more they can do. Dale and Kelly had reached that point.

As for the relationship between the three sisters, it was often confrontational, competitive, and even vindictive. Of course, anytime you have three, the old two-against-one strategy gets played. Their mother learned long ago to stay out of this game, as the two-against-one can quickly turn to three against mom.

CHAPTER 5: OUT OF THE GATES

RETURNING TO TRADITION WITHOUT the youngest Kenwood came with varying degrees of difficulty for each family member. There was a real struggle between moving on without Bobby, versus the thought of moving on in his memory.

In the garage at 2021 Seacliff Drive, Mr. Kenwood was using the early morning hours of December 23rd to prepare for their trip. This included the installation of a ski rack to the roof of his brand new European SUV. Once that was completed, two pairs of Italian snow skis were strapped down. Finally, a long cylindrical tube that housed a fishing pole was also affixed to the new rack. The skis belonged to Dale and Kelly and the fishing pole was to be a Christmas gift for Grandpa, a very expensive graphite Sierra XR-3. This would replace the fishing pole he was currently using that had been broken and fixed with duct tape several times.

Inside the rear portion of the SUV, behind the third-row seat, the girl's snowboards were neatly stacked alongside their snow gear. Tucked away in one corner was Dale's small (carry on size) suitcase. Stepping back, he admired his wonderful pack job thus far, and the ample room left for the rest of the family's suitcases.

One by one the female travelers emerged from the house into the garage. Amber and her mother placed their bulging suitcases at the rear of the SUV. Meagan followed with her suitcase, garment bag, and hypoallergenic pillow. Ample room was beginning to look like not enough room, especially as Makayla now added her oversized suitcase, garment bag, pink make-up case and a very large odd shaped black plastic bag.

"No, no, no, no... this is not going to fit" the head packer announced.

"But Dad, we need all our stuff" Makayla demanded.

She even had the audacity to suggest that maybe her father could use a smaller suitcase. He glanced over at his small carry-on, then turned his attention to the large odd shaped black plastic bag. When he asked what was inside, Makayla revealed that it was her latest first place trophy.

"I just know Grandma will want to see it in person" she stated with pride.

Standing almost two feet tall, the golden three-tiered jealousy maker came from a beauty pageant sponsored by the South Coast Animal Shelter. Winning first place also came with the honor of Makayla's image being used on a promotional campaign called: (EVERY DOG NEEDS A BEST FRIEND!).

Her father thought for one very short second before replying, "Hmm...yaah no, the trophy stays."

Next on the chopping block was the pink makeup case, deemed non-essential.

"But dad, I need my makeup case".

"Yeah dad," Meagan sarcastically agreed, "There might be a dog show in Oregon she can enter."

"You're just jealous."

"And you're just ugly."

By the time the key was in the ignition, Amber was taking sides, and by the time they were backing out of the garage, Kelly was refereeing. Even four females fighting to be heard could not drown out the loud scraping sound from above. Two pair of skis flew over the hood and across the garage floor landing next to the trophy. Apparently, the head packer made a height miscalculation with the new ski rack. With both shattered skis now safely in the garage, the door was shut.

"Guess you're leaving your skis behind too," Makayla remarked, still smarting over her trophy being left behind.

Her comment was ignored by her father, good thing, as space had just opened up on the rack above. Based on Dale's demeanor, it was probably best that nothing more was said about the garage incident. As he drove through the neighborhood a white fiberglass residue from the shattered skies blew across the hood, and stuck to the front window. Using the windshield wipers only made the situation worse. Unable to see through the smeared glass, another miscalculation was made. This time not with height, but distance. Misjudging their approach to the community's front gate resulted in Dale stomping on the brakes. This in turn had more than just the passengers launching forward. Apparently, the previous garage incident had compromised the lid on the tube which was still attached to the rack. As a result, Grandpa's fishing pole was launched through the air like a dispatched missile. Fortunately, gate guard Matt Williams was able to avoid being hit by the airborne projectile. Picking up the broken pieces of the graphite pole, Matt ran them up to the driver's door.

"Mr. K, were you planning on doing a little fishing, were you?" he asked.

An unwelcomed voice from the second row seat joked, "Yeah, fly fishing."

Laughter broke out inside the SUV, except for the driver, and the gate guard who remained professional. Matt actually complimented Mr. Kenwood on his fine choice of the Graphite Sierra XR-3.

"I've dreamed of owning one of these," he remarked.

"Well it's yours, all three pieces."

"Why thank you Mr. K, I think with a little duct tape, it'll be as good as new."

With two pair of skis and a fishing pole lighter, the Kenwoods were finally on their way north. Seven hours later, they were creeping along in San Francisco's bumper to bumper traffic. This is usually where the driver would find himself in a dilemma over whether to go right, left or stay in the undecided lane. Bay area commuters have no tolerance for last minute lane changes. As luck would have it, getting stuck in the right lane instead of the left lane left him right where he didn't want to go, downtown San Francisco. For the next forty minutes they were held captive to the city. Stop light–Starbucks–off ramp–stop light–Starbucks–off ramp. "WHERE THE HELL IS THE ON RAMP?" Dale yelled as he unsuccessfully dodged a pot hole.

This was actually the second time he hit this same pot hole and the second time he splashed mud on the same Salvation Army bell ringer on the corner. As Dale drove off, the angry man heaved his bell, narrowly missing the SUV. It bounced on the roadway in front of them and just like the pot hole, Dale was unsuccessful in dodging the shiny silver bell. A loud crunching sound was heard, followed by a few choice words from the now belless-bell-ringer. Kelly warned her husband that he better not pass by this same corner again.

"You think!" Dale uttered under his breath.

If he was going to escape, it meant doing something creative, possibly even something illegal. On their third rotation, Dale took a right turn on a left turn only, heading the wrong way down a one-way alley. Zig-zagging around graffiti tagged garbage bins and abandoned shopping carts, they eventually reached the other end. Blocking their exit though, was an intoxicated gentleman who had just finished relieving himself. Once he was zipped up, a $10.00 exit toll was paid, and Dale zipped out...

His paid escape actually paid off, as there it was, one the city's rare and elusive on ramps. Dale quickly crossed over a barrier curb, made an illegal U-turn and without using his blinker, merged back onto the freeway. With no flashing red light in the rearview mirror, it was smooth sailing all the way to the Golden Gate Bridge. There was, however, one more toll to be paid before leaving San Francisco. Fortunately, the man at the toll booth only had his hand out.

If ever a bridge separated two different worlds, the Gold Gate would be that bridge. Big city congestion on one shore and the laid-back village of Sausalito on the other. Like past years, the Kenwoods would spend December the 23rd here on the shores of the San Francisco Bay.

Sausalito's Shoreline Avenue runs parallel with a pedestrian trail that meanders the rocky edge of the salty waters. To the other side of the avenue are the quaint little boutiques, five-star hotels and restaurants with reputations. Part of the Kenwoods' yearly tradition was to stay one night at the historic SEA-YOUR-WAY-INN.

It didn't take long for the family to get settled into their two-bedroom one bath cottage, nor for the infamous battle over the mirror to begin. Four females fighting for time in front of one small mirror meant a long wait before heading out to dinner. By the time the females were ready, Dale was laid out on the sofa, half comatose from a toxic mix of hair spray and nail polish. The three block walk in the salty air to Sonetti's Ristorante, would certainly help clear his lungs.

Dinner at the five-star restaurant was another of the family's traditions. Owners, Mario and Annie Sonetti, had become good friends of the Kenwoods over the years. They were both anxiously expecting the Kenwoods tonight.

"I have-a your table for-a-six all-a-ready for you," Mario stated in his heavy accent.

This caught the Kenwoods a bit off guard. The Sonettis were well aware of Bobby's passing, even making the trip to L.A. two years ago to attend his memorial service. So why the six place settings? Further confusion came as the family noticed that the menus were embossed with Bobby's name. For a brief moment, no one said anything. Each member of the family took time to read the front cover of tonight's special menu. Underneath Bobby's name was a notation that read: "All proceeds from tonight's dinners will be donated to Cancer Research".

"I believe Bobarino's-a-here with us tonight," Mario proclaimed. He then took a moment to reminisce, remembering two years back when Bobby had asked why he always wore a red rose on his lapel. That night, Mario had explained to him that the rose was a symbol of love.

"When I wear-a-the rose, I share-a that love with-a everyone," he had told Bobby.

Mario was now joined by his wife, Annie. She carefully removed the rose from his lapel. They each took turns kissing the petals, before placing the rose upon the table in front of the empty seat. Then together, they performed the sign of the cross, followed by a brief moment of silence. Tears ran down Mario's cheeks, which he wiped away before anyone noticed. Turning towards his head waiter, he loudly clapped his hands above his head, yelling out, " GIUSEPPE, THIS IS-A BOBBARINO'S FAMILY...THEY-A-HUNGRY...BRING-A BREAD".

For a brief moment the family sat silently, again looking at the very special menus before them. Meagan excused herself from the table in the same manner she usually did, by just leaving and saying nothing. Her parents watched as she walked over to the large window next to the host stand. In the past, Bobby and Mario had stood together there, gazing out across the bay. It was now Meagan who joined the impeccably dressed restauranteur at the window. There was not much to see though, as the fog was thick and heavy across the bay.

"Your brother, he a like-a-the stars" he told her.

As the two stood side by side, Mario shared another memory about her little brother, something Bobby shared the last time they were together. Mario recalled how they were standing exactly where Meagan and he now stood, looking up at the sky that night.

"Bobby, your-a brother, he say to me, only one thing looks better in the dark. I ask him, what's-a-that? He say to me that night ... "THE STARS OF COURSE."

Just as Mario said this, the two watched in awe as the existing curtain of fog was pulled out to sea. It wasn't instant, rather smooth and gradual, exposing more and more with each passing moment. At first, the arched span of the Golden Gate appeared out of the gray. A stream of white lights moving in one direction, and red in the other. As the fog continued to lift, the lights of San Francisco were exposed. A million lights, doubled by their reflection in the bay...and then, the grand finale so to speak. A dull gray sky gave way to a vast blackness filled with sparkling stars. Mario placed his hand upon Meagan's frail shoulder and spoke.

"Your-a-brother, he was-a right about those stars...yes?"

Nothing more was said between the two. Meagan just slowly pulled away and returned to the dinner table. Giuseppe was in the process of taking orders. For the next hour, plates of pasta were enjoyed by all, except for Meagan. She chose to nibble on a Caesar salad minus the anchovies and croutons. Before the family headed back to their cottage, they took a few minutes to enjoy the company of their friends. Mario even sang an old Italian Christmas song about a donkey while Annie played the accordion.

Walking back to the cottage, the family passed by the same nostalgic establishments that had been there year after year, such as the corner lingerie store with the pink and white striped awnings. Over the years, the mannequins' undergarments had become smaller and smaller with bigger and bigger price tags, most likely the effects of global warming and inflation.

All of a sudden Amber began to laugh out loud as they passed by the shop. Her mind flashed back to two years prior. She reminded the family about the time Bobby ran into the lingerie store asking the clerk where the candy was located. At the time, the family was embarrassed by this incident. Now, two years later, they were able to laugh about it as they passed by the lingerie store named 'Eye Candy'.

Further down the street, they passed by 77 Shore Line Avenue, home of Guido's Cup of Joe. For years, this had been the last hold out from Sausalito's former fishing village era. Quaint and nostalgic, it had a special sentimental charm to Dale.

"Look Dad, your crappy old coffee shop is gone," Amber called out.

For thirteen years, Mr. Kenwood had purchased Christmas Eve morning coffee and donuts at Guido's. In fact, the owner had become a friend of sorts. While the rest of the family would sleep in, Dale would slip out for coffee and conversation with Guido himself. The old red florescent sign that had always glowed in the morning fog, was now gone. In its place was a fancy new sign that read, "Miranda's Higher Ground–Coffee Lounge".

Peering in through the suede curtain lined windows, Dale discovered nothing was the same. With his hands cupped against the window, he looked in like a sad little boy at a closed toy store. Everything he had come to love about his own personal morning tradition was gone. The row of old ripped vinyl bar stools where coffee and conversation with Guido took place ... gone. The cracked Formica counter top ... gone. The photographs of fishermen and their catch of the day ... all gone. Even the old port hole door was no more. Looking in, he now saw leather sofas and chairs, granite counter tops, and modern cobalt blue drop lighting. Where old black and white photographs had once hung, there were now abstract paintings framed and for sale.

At the former Guido's Cup of Joe, coffee came served in Styrofoam cups. Your only choice was the size: Dinghy, Tug, or Tanker. In layman's terms: Large – extra-large or hand over an entire pot. There were donuts too, Guido's batch of the day... usually plain or glazed. At the new Miranda's, there was an entire chalk board filled with menu items. Fun foods and dazzling drinks were spelled out in fancy fluorescent colored fonts with names like Cable Car Cappuccino, Golden Gate Ground, Lombard Lemon Bars and so on and so forth. Tomorrow morning would be a real interesting twist to an old tradition.

Upon returning to the cottage, the two youngest girls slipped right into bed. On the sofa opposite of where Dale now sat tending to the fire, Meagan pretended to already be asleep. She did so to avoid sharing a room with her sisters.

"Are you coming to bed? " Kelly asked her husband from the second bedroom's doorway.

Instead of answering her question, he made a comment that brought her to his side.

"Bobby sure would have loved those menus...with his...you know...name and all..."

She began to rub his shoulders in hopes of coaxing him to open up about their son. Two years had now gone by since Bobby's passing and Dale had yet to share his heart. Tonight, his comment did little to change that fact, but what it did do was open the door. After sitting quietly for a few minutes together, Kelly kissed his cheek and went off to bed.

Only a faint warm glow filled the room where Dale now sat alone in front of the fire. Across from him, his eldest daughter still pretending to be asleep. With one eye slightly open, she watched as her father pulled out a small photograph from his wallet. Clutching it in both hands, she noticed the fires reddish glow reflected in a tear that rolled down his cheek. Somewhere deep inside of her she longed to comfort her father. Instead, Meagan just rolled over, convinced that a daughter's attention could never comfort a father's tears for his son.

CHAPTER 6: ONE MAN TWO JOURNEYS

CHRISTMAS EVE MORNING CAME with Dale off to discover a new tradition. Miranda's open sign glowed in the morning fog, welcoming the early morning crowd. To his surprise, the new owner was actually someone he had met several times before, Guido's only daughter, twenty-seven-year-old Deanna. Right away, the conversation turned to that of a question about her father's whereabouts. That's when Dale learned about Guido's unfortunate passing. A polite inquiry was made for further details on this shocking news. Since customers were already pouring in, she asked that Mr. Kenwood follow her into a back room.

Entering through the swinging doors at the rear of Miranda's was like stepping back in time. There before him were the old Formica counter tops and vinyl bar stools. Even the old fishing photos from years gone by were now on display, one room from where they originally hung.

"Dad's friends still prefer to sit back here," she told Dale.

Deanna then shared briefly about how her father had died in an accident eighteen months earlier. Sitting on one of the vinyl bar stools, anger came over Dale as he intently listened. Apparently, Guido and an employee by the name of Race had shot over to San Francisco to pick up supplies, followed by attending a football game. After the 49ers won in overtime, the two indulged in a few celebratory beers. On the drive back, Guido slept in the passenger seat and an intoxicated Race took the wheel. That night a thick fog rolled across the Golden Gate. Six divided lanes were swallowed up in a grey mist, resulting in a collision. The wife of a local pastor had little chance against the delivery van as it veered directly into her lane.

"My father and Mrs. Sanchez both died on scene," she told Dale.

Condolences were the first words out of his mouth, followed up by a question as to the intoxicated driver's punishment. Deanna reluctantly shared how Race ended up receiving four months in jail after spending three months in the hospital.

"GOOD!" Dale replied, "I hope he spent that time thinking about his carless actions!"

Obviously, Dale was assuming Deanna felt the same way. However, her response did not support that assumption.

"I can assure you, Race lives with his mistake" she replied.

"Well good, I have no tolerance for mistakes like that...NONE."

Deanna sensed that Dale's reaction over her father's accident was about something far more personal. It was quite obvious his resentment came from something from his own past. She sympathized with him somewhat, as eighteen months earlier, she dealt with similar emotions. Deanna felt called to share a piece of wisdom with her father's friend.

"My pastor once told me that forgiveness is as much for the forgiver as it is for the forgiven." She paused for a second before adding, "This only made sense to me after I chose to forgive Race."

She returned to the front of the shop after making this comment. It was strange how she chose to focus on forgiveness, something Dale struggled with more than anything else. Just the mere idea of forgiving the man that caused his son Bobby's death, was to him, inconceivable.

Passing back through the swinging doors, an old tradition was left behind. Miranda's was now bustling with employees and customers. It took a while, but eventually Dale had his order in hand. As he prepared to leave, he heard Deanna yell out to her staff, "has anyone seen my husband?"

"He's in the bakery with Miranda," a voice yelled out.

Hearing this, Dale put off leaving for the moment. His curiosity was peaked, wanting to see the shops namesake, not to mention Deanna's husband. As a female employee passed by, Dale leaned in and asked her, "So who is Miranda?"

"Deanna's baby girl" she replied.

"Ohhhhhh, so the shop is named after Guido's granddaughter".

"Well, yes and no. The shop is named after Pastor Sanchez's late wife, and baby Miranda is named after her"

Just then, a man in a wheel chair with a little girl sitting on his lap came through the bakery doors. The employee pointed the two out. "There's Miranda now".

As the two rolled by, Dale heard another employee call out to the man in the wheel chair, "Hey Race, your wife is looking for you."

It took a few seconds for all the pieces to fall into place. Deanna, the pastor, Race, and forgiveness, all fantastic and fine for them. For Dale, and his situation, he could never consider forgiveness. He'd rather hold on to his anger and resentment. Even his mother-in-law, Betty, had tried to convince him

41

otherwise, telling him that resentment is like hitting your own thumb with a hammer and expecting it to hurt the other person. Apparently this didn't resonate with Dale, not one bit. Over the last two years, he chose a hammer over forgiveness.

Once back at the cottage, the females enjoyed their food while at the same time fighting for time in front of the mirror. For the next forty minutes, Dale sat alone on the sofa sipping his Cable Car coffee as he waited. His mind flashed back to exactly two years ago to this very day. That Christmas Eve morning he and Bobby sat on the very same sofa waiting on the girls to get ready.

"Such a waste of our time," Dale remembered saying.

Bobby had quickly disagreed with him replying, "I don't think it's a waste of time, you know why?"

At this point in the flashback, Dale began to get choked up. He remembered how his son was sitting beside him, seemingly happy and content. His little body still bloated from past chemo and his face still swollen and red.

"Why?" Dale had asked.

Bobby smiled and replied, "Because silly...I get you all to myself."

Snapping out of his flashback, Dale retrieved a medication bottle from his coat pocket. He quickly removed the lid pouring four pills into his hand. Two were put into his pants pocket and the other two quickly swallowed down. This was done just as the howl of hairdryers came to an end. The females emerged from the bathroom, all packed and ready to go.

Once back on the road north, the salty air gradually gave way to the earthy sweet smell of the grape-growing vineyards of the Napa Valley. Award winning wineries dot both sides of the road until the dairy farms take over. Besides milk, these cows produce another byproduct that dot the roadside. This part of the drive always placed the Kenwoods within a family debate, windows up or windows down. Neither ever worked. For the driver, it was a great excuse to speed through the area.

"SLOW DOWN!" Kelly yelled, "do you want another speeding ticket?" This was followed by 'the old double our insurance lecture' and the threat of driving school.

Before long they entered into the Humboldt Forest. The road narrowed under the dark canopy of the giant Sequoias, ancient trees that encroached upon the twisted road like living guard rails. Many of them were scarred by past accidents. Maneuvering through the twists and turns was not a problem for Dale, his weakness after all was with heights, for example, garage doors. Gripping the SUV's leather wrapped steering wheel, there was not much that could interfere with his precision driving except...those uttered three words, "I'm car sick." With nowhere to pull over, at least not right away ... it happened. With one loud guttural sound, the smell of fine Italian leather was replaced by the smell of last night's Italian dinner. At this point, there was no debating about it. All agreed, windows down.

A safe place was finally found to pull over. Dale cleaned his leather seat and headrest, while Kelly cleaned the back of his head. Once back on the road, forty miles of fresh air had the incident all but forgotten. Not far ahead, in the middle of nowhere, was another of the Kenwoods' traditions. Lunch at a unique place named after an elusive ape-like creature, one that roams in the deep dark shadows of the Sequoias. Locals call him Big Foot. Some have heard his eerie late night screams, while others have stumbled across a set of his enormous

footprints...... and then ... there are those who have actually survived an eyewitness encounter. Some have even captured indisputable proof in a photograph. Inside the museum, next to

Big Foot Burgers, you can view these blurry black and white photos for yourself.

Rounding one of the many curves on this highway, there is no possible way to miss this unique roadside eatery and museum. Their signage is a twenty-foot tall wood carving of Big Foot himself. This one-star restaurant prides itself on quantity of food over quality. Following the cement footprint castings that serve as stepping stones, you are lead to the front door of this unique restaurant. Three converted box cars make up the dining area, and a caboose can be reserved for small catered weddings.

Across the parking lot is a vintage thirty-five foot air stream trailer. Many are fooled by the rusty exterior, but inside is the world's finest collection of Big Foot artifacts. Unlike traditional museums, items can be obtained by simply making a twenty-five dollar donation. Doing so, you will receive an actual strand of Big Foot hair sealed in a glass vile. Handmade souvenirs can also be purchased. For a mere one hundred dollars, the museum's curator himself will step outside, fire up his chainsaw, and instantly carve something unique out of a log.

Eating here at Big Foot Burgers was a Kenwood tradition quite different from that of dining at Sonetti's. Here, menus and manners do not exist. Belching is considered a compliment to the chef and any other bodily noises, merely a side effect from the food. The signature burger, measuring eighteen inches across, is one of only two menu items. As the legend goes, this enormous size is based on an actual Big Foot scat pile found about a mile north. Certainly not an appetizing fact, but neither is the story behind the bucket of chili. Portions of this size are meant to be enjoyed by an entire family or, let's say, a log tossing team. With that said, any individual finishing an entire bucket of chili in ten minutes or less, eats for free. Not

 JAMES D. APPLEGATE

to mention, their name is added to the Hall of Fame board just outside the restrooms.

Pulling into Big Foot's parking lot posted as "Carnivore Parking Only" Kelly and her vegetarian daughter were already at battle. Meagan demanded to stay in the SUV where she planned to sleep in the third row seat.

"I have my own food," she yelled from beneath her blanket.

To be fair, this was not really the type of restaurant that catered to Meagan's kind. Even the sign that hung in the front window wasn't all that inviting, "Vegetarians are a BIG-MISSED STEAK." Forgoing a fight, Meagan was left to sleep in the third row seat. When the family did return, their grunts and groans did not wake the teen. Back on the road heading north it didn't take long for the rest of the passengers to fall asleep, including the co-pilot. Speed was now under Dale's full control. That is, until Amber began complaining about her stomach. Her loud moans woke both Makayla and her mother.

"Slow down," Kelly ordered, "you're making everyone sick!"

"Should I trade seats with Amber, since I already got sick in this one?" Makayla kindly offered.

This was followed by a loud sound coming from Amber.

"Never mind, too late," Makayla remarked holding her nose.

If Dale didn't already have reason enough to pull over, then the flashing red lights in his rear view mirror gave him enough. Trying to find a safe place to pull over wasn't easy, especially while receiving the old double our insurance lecture. "Hope you like traffic school," Kelly uttered under her breath. Dale watched in the rear view mirror as the officer made his approach. He noticed that he stopped for a moment at the back of the vehicle.

"Say honey, did you put the new license plates on the car like I asked?" Dale's question was quite clear and yet, Kelly's silence was even clearer.

A very large officer now stood outside of the driver's door with one hand resting upon his revolver.

"You folks missing something?" he asked in a very harsh tone.

"Yes officer. That would be my fault" Kelly admitted from the passenger seat. "I realized I forgot once we were on the road, and well, I didn't want to make my husband turn around … you understand ...right?"

"Lady, we don't take kindly to abandoning children around here!"

"Wait ...what... ABANDON". All at once, five sets of eyes turned towards the back of the SUV. There in the third row seat was a blanket, a hypoallergenic pillow, but no sleeping teen.

"Someone stole Meagan," Makayla screamed.

"No little girl, your parents left her back at Big Foot Burgers," the officer stated.

Kelly frantically explained to the officer about their misunderstanding. Within minutes, the Kenwoods were heading south with a police escort. Returning to the scene of the abandonment, they noticed a large crowd had gathered. Meagan quickly slithered through the beef eating bystanders, jumped into the third row seat, and covered herself with her blanket. Nothing was said by the teen for now. Both parents thanked the officers for their help and their understanding.

For the second time in the last ninety minutes, the Kenwoods, including Meagan this time, left Big Foot Burgers parking lot heading north. Bouncing back onto the highway, a very angry third row seat passenger now rose up to vent.

"I can NOT believe you left me at that disgusting place."

"We thought you were sleeping," Kelly replied.

Meagan explained how she was trying to use the bathroom, but three of the four toilets were clogged and she had to wait for the other one that was in the process of being clogged.

"Well again, we thought you were sleeping and didn't want to wake you."

"UGGH ... I HATE EVERYONE!"

With that, Meagan retreated back into hiding under her blanket. This little setback, so to speak, put the Kenwoods behind schedule. That meant a phone call to advise the grand-parents was in order. Unfortunately, Bill answered Kelly's call at the same time the answering machine kicked on. Father and daughter tried their best to communicate while Betty's pre-re-corded voice talked over them.

"How do I get your mother to stop talking on this thing?" her frustrated 87 year-old father yelled into the receiver.

Two attempts were made to explain how to shut off the machine, to no avail.

"This contraption has NEVER worked right," her father firmly stated.

For the next ten minutes Kelly leaned back in her seat, rub-bing her forehead while she listened to her father's latest gripes. She never even had a chance to address the reason for the call.

Her father ranted right up until he had to hang up. Apparently, his favorite radio show was about to start. A special Christmas Eve edition, "How the Dems Stole Christmas."

"Got to go," he said before the phone went dead.

Shaking her head back and forth, Kelly mumbled out the same words she commonly did after a conversation with her father, "I need a drink..."

After giving his wife a few seconds to do her breathing exercises, Dale then asked, "Ok, let's have it?"

"Well... let's see...Dad would like the receipt for the answering machine we got him twelve years ago. Apparently, he would like to return it since it's broken."

"Maybe he can fix it with some of his duct tape," Dale joked.

"Oh wait, it gets better. The CD player we sent them last Christmas ... he would like to return that too, since it broke the first time he used it."

"I thought we sent a DVD player."

"We did."

Over the next few miles, conversation slowly gave way to silence, and the rain to snow. Each of the passengers eventually fell off to sleep. Dale was making great time until getting stuck behind a truck and trailer hauling four snowmobiles. This triggered yet another flashback, a memory of the day his son was fatally hit by a snowmobile. Emotions began to surface, which had Dale digging into his pants pocket, retrieving the two pills he had put there earlier. With the last of his Cable Car coffee, they were quickly swallowed down.

Up ahead was Tragedy Springs Road, the last off-ramp before heading up into the wilderness of the Siskiyous. As the driver of the truck in front of him slowed to take the off-ramp, Dale accelerated around him missing the road closure sign that was just being set up.

Passing through the yet to be closed gates, it didn't take long before the falling snow transformed the road from black to white. Conditions already warranted that the four wheel drive be engaged. Looking in his rear view mirror, Dale noticed no headlights from behind. After almost thirty minutes on the road, he passed no vehicles coming down the mountain. This should have worried him ...

CHAPTER 7: STRANDED

LOOKING OUT FROM HIS office window, Warden Ridge McCallister was not so worried about the gray sky above. It was the ominous black sky moving in from the north that was concerning. The 3:15 pm release time could not come soon enough. Since changing the departure time was not an option, McCallister focused on making sure everything and everybody was ready on the hour. At 3 pm, the old Dodge van was chained up and idling on the cobblestone drive in front of the Tunnel Creek Prison. In the driver's seat Landon adjusted his seat-belt while his fellow guard, Mark Smith, buckled in a huge Christmas basket on the front passenger seat.

"We decided the Mayor's basket should go with you this year," Smith remarked.

For the self-proclaimed foodie in the driver's seat, it was a gift he accepted graciously. Landon was probably the only one who would willingly eat food prepared by the domestically challenged Mayor's wife, Carol. Of course, anyone who ate week old Sushi from Tomahawk Tom's gas station probably wouldn't balk at a basket of bad baked goods.

At 3:10 pm, passenger BC was sliding into the back seat alongside his camouflage duffel bag.

"Welcome to Gertrude," Landon greeted him.

"Excuse me."

"Gertrude! That's the name I've given this van," he replied with a great big smile. "It was also the name of my third wife's mother. This bucket of bolts reminds me of her".

"How's that?" the young man questioned.

"Well let's see... they're both big... old... and ugly, and I'll be damned if either won't drive you away" ...and with that said, Gertrude was shoved into gear.

Standing just outside the passenger side of the van next to Smith was the warden himself. He did something he had never done before. McCallister handed his former inmate a small neatly wrapped package. He then stepped back, stood tall, and held a salute until the van faded into a haze of lightly falling snow. Reaching the gate at the end of the cobblestone drive, a new beginning awaited BC on the other side.

Gate guard, Mary Andrews, could not help but notice the Christmas basket on the front passenger seat, prompting her to ask, "Who's that for?"

"It's mine!" Landon replied. "We all got a basket with our Christmas bonus checks this morning."

Until this very moment, Mary had no idea of her financial windfall. For a second or two her mind escaped to a happy place, but as the van pulled away, she snapped out of her designer handbag hysteria, calling out to Landon, "wait ... how much ... how much is the bonus?"

With no reply, her head popped out of the guard booth like a spring-loaded jack in the box yelling, "WHERE DO I GET MY BONUS?" Landon again did not reply nor even slow down, leaving her no choice but to race out of the booth flailing her hands in the air in an attempt to get his attention. Her final words came as she slid across the ice on her back side, "Where do I get my bonus?"

Landon had no time to answer questions. Between watching Mary's Ice Capades in the rearview mirror and laughing uncontrollably, it was all he could do just keep Gertrude on the highway.

"I bet she calls HR right now," Landon remarked to his back seat passenger. "Where's my basket? Where's my Christmas bonus?"

"Is there a bonus?" BC asked.

"Are you kidding, we work for Uncle Scrooge."

"Then why would you trick your friend like that?"

"First of all, Mary is no friend. She's one of my ex-wives," Landon fired back. "Secondly, that is called spreading Christmas cheer, something we all need more of my friend."

"I don't get it. How is that spreading Christmas cheer?"

Landon turned his head, exposing a great big cheesy grin, "See...see how cheerful that made me."

From that point on, conversation occupied most of their time on the road. Even though the two had known each other for 24 months, talk between prisoners and guards was regulated. Beyond the walls of Tunnel Creek though, no topic was off limits, and so the two shared openly and freely with one another. Almost right away they discovered some unique similarities, not the kind that are superficial or funny, but the kind that build bonds through personal understanding. For instance, they discovered they both grew up without the benefit of a family. Even though Landon lived with his biological father for a time, he supplied nothing more than a home filled with anger and hate. There was never enough money for essentials, and yet always enough for alcohol and cigarettes. Landon couldn't even count on there being food in the home, and if he complained, a beating usually ensued.

"It's weird," he told BC with an uncomfortable chuckle. "All I wanted as a child was to be loved, and now I run from it."

Even though Landon opened up about his abuse, BC did not. He hinted about it, but it was a different kind of abuse, the kind most men find hard to talk about. Just the fact they shared what they did, was quite amazing. It brought both to the realization that their imperfect childhoods had an effect on their adult lives. Both admittedly had problems with relationships. Landon was the classic runner, BC, the avoider. Two hours in a van together and the beginnings of a friendship took shape.

Before long, they entered the last little town nestled at the foot of the Siskiyou Mountains. Pine Bluff was already covered in newly fallen snow. Christmas lights outlined the town architecture and coiled up every street light down Main Street. The town's crowning jewel was a huge star that hung suspended between the courthouse and the Pine Bluff Baptist Church. After a quick fuel stop, the two were headed up the summit. Where Main Street ended, the dark steep road of Devil's Slide began. Looking out the vans side window, BC watched as the lights of the last decorated farmhouse faded into the winter landscape.

Grinding upward, the van's engine howled as it was dropped into second gear. Only two headlights shined the way through the twisty turns leading higher and deeper into the dark wilderness. From the opposing lane covered in white, not one vehicle came down from above. Though Landon displayed little concern, it was apparent to him that the storm had shown up unpredictably early. There would be no further vehicles to follow in their tracks, as the gates behind them were now closed.

The chained tires of the old van, chiseled through the icy snow leaving tracks that vanished within minutes after being laid. Backseat spectator, BC, could only watch as Landon's driving skills were on display. From the driver's seat, an impressive repetitive performance was underway...soft break–turn–acceleration–soft break–turn–acceleration, and so on and so on. With each mile upward the storm claimed a little more of the road. Snow covered pines lined the thin white path that Landon skillfully threaded them through. After thirty minutes of intense driving the summit lied just ahead. This is where the climb would come to an end and the treacherous decline would begin.

From the opposite direction there was only one vehicle making the climb from the California side. About a mile ahead Dale was dealing with the same winter conditions. Remarkably relaxed, he maneuvered through the terrain while his passengers all slept.

Meanwhile in the van, each gust of wind brought a chill whistling through the weathered rubber seals of the windows. Since the only heating vents were on the dash, Landon made a suggestion.

"Why don't you trade places with the basket and sit up here like a grownup."

Accepting the offer, BC grabbed the Christmas basket and set it next to his duffel bag. Placing his outstretched leg over the front seat he prepared to make the move forward.

"HOLD ON! " Landon yelled.

Two dim headlights appeared out of nowhere heading straight for the old van. Landon had no choice but to yank the wheel towards the shoulder. This aggressive move sent the unbuckled passenger flying back to the second-row seat. The other vehicle made no attempt to stop or return to their lane. To prevent a head-on collision, Landon continued to steer towards the shoulder. Just before they nose dived off the highway, the other vehicle brushed across the vans rear bumper. The impact awoke all four passengers, not to mention the driver, before spinning out.

Apparently, Dale had dozed off, resulting in two vehicles to now plummet off the road. Fortunately for the Kenwoods, their vehicle only took out a road sign before coming to a powdery stop within a snow bank. Daughter by daughter, the parents discovered that their children survived the crash unscathed. At this point, the passengers had no idea what caused the accident, but Dale knew very well it was his fault. He also held full responsibility for the fate of those in the other vehicle. As much as he hated to leave his family alone, he knew what he had to do.

Prior to heading out, Dale tried unsuccessfully to restart the stalled-out engine. No engine meant no heat, and no heat meant no time to waste. Bundled up as best he could, his exit came through the rear hatch since all four doors were buried window-high in snow.

As he left armed with only a flashlight, the last bit of heat escaped with him. Fighting for each step he took, he headed in the direction where he believed the other vehicle left the road. Moving fast was essential, as the storm was quickly taking any signs of the tracks. Only minutes into his search, he caught a glimpse of the van's tail lights about twenty feet down a ravine. Sliding most of the way down, he was met by the two men who now stood outside the wreckage. It was quickly shared that no one had been injured in either vehicle. Even standing just feet apart, their conversation had to be yelled over the storm's howls. Introduction were followed by Dale admitting he had fallen asleep at the wheel. He tried to apologize but Landon interrupted him.

"It was an accident, leave it at that!"

He then proceeded to shine his flashlight into the van, revealing a large tree limb that had crashed through the front window piercing the passenger seat. It was only by God's grace that BC had not been sitting there at the time. As it was, the compromised old van would play no part in their survival. Each swirl of wind blanketed the interior with freezing snow. It was decided they would all seek shelter in the Kenwood's SUV. It would be tight quarters for seven individuals, but when your options total one, that's the one you go with.

Wasting no time, the two men gathered up their duffle bags along with the Christmas basket, and headed up the ravine. One by one, they resurfaced onto the highway, which incidentally now resembled a groomed ski run. Every tire track or trace of his recently laid footprints had been erased by the storm. Each gust of wind came with a disorienting swirl of change. Walking the highway's edge, the men played a life or death game of Hide-n-go-seek. Dale's worried state quickly turned to panic. Minutes passed before Landon's flashlight caught the faint reflection of something laying on a snow bank. Closer inspection revealed it was the road sign that denoted their current ridge top location of" Unforgiven Point ". The freshly broken post and sign were just the clues Landon needed. Twenty feet further, he stumbled upon the back end of the SUV.

"OVER HERE...OVER HERE!"

Within seconds, BC alongside a very relieved Dale Kenwood, joined Landon at the rear of the vehicle. Getting out of the elements took precedent over introductions. All non-essential items were quickly tossed out to make room for the two additional men. Dale entered first, joining his family in the front two seats. BC stated he would take the smaller rear section. Standing beneath the hatch as Landon hopped in was not the best idea. Two hundred and seventy five pounds sent the hatch door dropping down upon BC's head, not a hard hit, but enough to send him backwards into a snow bank. Stunned more than anything else, it took a few seconds to compose himself. During this brief moment, sight was regained in his left eye, the very same one that was blinded by shrapnel in Afghanistan. For one fleeting second, he saw what looked like a shadowy outline of a man standing in the tree line. When he blinked, the sight in his left eye was once again gone. Gradually his right eye regained full vision, but what he thought he had seen was no longer there.

Just as BC was about to enter the SUV, a gust of wind struck his entire body. It was filled with pelting ice... and the faint hint of a smoke, like that produced by a fireplace. More likely than not, it was just the winter cold playing tricks on his mind. After all, the nearest chimney had to be more than twenty miles down the mountain. That didn't change the fact that his curiosity was provoked. Grabbing a flashlight, he kept the real reason for his quest secret, simply telling the others he would be right back. Through the frosted rear window, the others watched as the flashlight's beam of light disappeared into the storm.

Inside the SUV, the stranded could see their own breath as they made introductions and small talk. Plans on what to do to survive were delicately addressed next. Not much headway was made here as they had no options. After about five minutes, Kelly found herself unable to contain her concern over the young man out in the elements.

"Someone needs to go find him!" she blurted out.

"He's a former Marine ma'am, a military hero, he'll be fine," Landon assured her.

In an effort to take everyone's focus off the current situation, Landon quickly changed the topic. Since he had a discerning nose for all foods, he sniffed around the second row seat area several times and then shared his findings.

"If I'm not mistaken, I smell Italian food ...?"

"GROSS" Makayla blurted out.

"What, you don't like Italian food?"

"Not that kind!"

Once again, Kelly expressed her concern about the young man. At this point, it had been far too long. Landon now agreed, as he assumed BC had just taken a bathroom break.

"What is he doing" Landon uttered under his breath, "waiting for a roll of toilet paper and warm towelette."

Done with waiting, he prepared to go out in search of his new friend. Grunting his way to the rear hatch, the SUV rocked a little deeper into the snow. Just as he reached for the handle, the hatch opened from the outside. Standing before the freezing passengers was BC.....and he was not alone. Next to him was a giant man, his head a whole two feet above the open hatch. He wore a fur hat that covered the entirety of his forehead. From the top of his cheeks on down to his waistline, a bushy beard blew wildly in the wind. BC introduced him as Mr. Cartwright, the owner of a cabin just beyond the tree line.

"I have a fireplace and not much more, you're welcome to seek shelter there," the stranger told them.

"What, no hot tub!" Landon remarked. "I'm kidding, let's get the heck out of here."

Everyone quickly gathered their essentials and prepared to leave the freezer on wheels. As each person exited, they thanked the towering bearded stranger. Landon himself, who was 6'3" was quite a bit smaller, not so much horizontally, but vertically. In a matter of minutes, all eight were tromping through the snow, led by a man draped in a bearskin and balancing a Christmas basket on his head. Along the way, the only complainer was Makayla, who was swooped up by Landon, thrown over his shoulder and carried. Each bone chilling gust of wind fought against every step the stranded took. Their only chance at survival slowly came into view on the other side of a small meadow. Beneath three towering pines was a little cabin puffing out smoke from its rock chimney. Reaching the half-buried door, Mr. Cartwright pushed it open with his wood staff. As the door creaked open, the golden glow of a crackling fire came into view. Like ants to a freshly dropped crumb, the three girls and their mother headed straight for the fireplace.

There was no running water, electricity, or cell phone reception. Lighting was provided by the fire, and the fire was the only thing preventing anyone from freezing to death tonight. Standing in a half circle around the hearth, the fire gave each a chance to see one another clearly for the first time. Right away Makayla noticed Mr. Cartwright's eyes. They were a piercing solid white. She whispered to her father that she found his eyes to be scary-weird.

"I'm blind child, not deaf" Mr. Cartwright grumbled in a dry voice.

"If you're blind, how did you lead us here?" Amber asked.

"With my nose!"

"You can't see with a nose," Makayla fired back on Amber's behalf.

Mr. Cartwright explained how he used his nose to follow the smoke from the fireplace and, in essence, see his way back.

"I can also see that you are a bit presumptuous and that you recently ate Italian food that didn't agree with you, am I not right?" he asked.

Neither of the girls responded, partially because they were embarrassed, and neither had any idea what presumptuous meant.

"Are you alone out here?" Dale asked the bearded stranger.

"I was until you showed up."

"Sorry," Dale replied, "but as you know we had an accident"

"HUH, that was no accident."

"What do you mean by that?" Kelly asked calmly.

"It's my cabin ma'am and I will ask the questions, thank you very much!"

His reply made everyone a bit uncomfortable. Even though he was admittedly blind, he seemed to be glaring at Dale as if he knew he was the reason for the accident. In an effort to ease the tension for all, Landon tried to make nice.

"I, for one, want to thank Mr. Cartwright for opening his door to seven unexpected visitors on Christmas Eve."

"Unexpected?" the old cabin owner replied in a confrontational tone. "I have been expecting you all night!"

"I hardly doubt that" Landon hesitantly replied.

"Then why else would I be standing out in a blizzard for two hours?"

There was no answer to this question. Instead, the seven stranded started to wonder if maybe Mr. Cartwright was not playing with a full deck.

CHAPTER 8: MEAGAN AND THE STORM

A T THE BASE OF the mountain pass to either side, the road had now been closed for more than three hours. For the seven stranded, they were currently safe and warm, a comforting fact that could not be communicated to loves below. Even though the mountain top cabin had withstood years of winter storms, this might turn out to be the worst in its long history. Just to the other side of the front door, three towering pines swayed as if their trunks were made of rubber. Falling debris, ice and snow joined forces with the wind, pelting the aged wood exterior of the structure. Each blustery gust rocked the cabin at Unforgiven to its foundation.

From a window five thousand feet below, Bill and Betty Applegate stood together holding hands. Their eyes fixated on the dark snow-covered street, watching for the headlights of their long overdue loved ones. A feast still simmered in the kitchen as the centerpiece candles on the dining room table burned faint and low. Off in the distance, the muffled sound of the Pine Bluff Baptist Church bells could be heard. Christmas Eve service would be missed this year.

Up in the heart of the storm, the winter assault was in high gear. Landon tried his best to divert the young girl's attention from the relentless arctic winds pounding upon all four walls.

"Come over here," he called out to the three teens, "let me teach you something you"ll never learn in the city".

Amber and Makayla both joined him next to the fireplace. Meagan however, remained where she sat filing her nails in a dark corner of the cabin.

"There's an art to fire making," Landon remarked, as he positioned a log within. "Where most people might just toss another log on the fire, they would be wrong in doing so. Precise log placement is critical. Stack it wrong and your fire lacks the oxygen to breathe. Most important is the usage of properly aged wood."

Both of the girls showed little to no interest in what he was talking about. Since Landon wasn't accustomed to speaking to city girls, his topic was not the most engaging, and his choice of analogies not really age appropriate.

"Let's compare the wood to aged whiskey ... only with wood, you don't want to age it too long. Too dry, it will burn too fast. Likewise, if it's too green, it's like a cheap bottom shelf whiskey, the fire's gonna spit it up."

"Hey mister, guess what?" Makayla interrupted. "We don't care. Our fireplace at home has metal logs."

"...and we don't drink," Amber added.

Landon's diversion of whisky and wood failed miserably. Just as he was about move on to his knowledge of beer making and log tossing, a wind gust struck the cabin at Unforgiven with such force that the main support beam made a loud cracking sound. Every wooden slat in the four walls rattled around the stranded. Each gust came with more strength than the last, and more frequent. A direct hit from above sent some of the cement mortar from the rock chimney falling down upon the flames. Tending to the fire was one thing. As for the structure itself, it was at the mercy of the storm. At any given point, the one thing that separated them from certain death could be taken away.

"Are we going to die?" the frightened middle child asked.

Before either parent could attempt to hand out comforting assurances that no one was going to die, the eldest daughter spoke her mind. Her words were harsh. Several years of oppressed resentment hidden up until now, were shared in the face of possible death.

"You think they really care?...well they don't," Meagan assured her sisters.

Caught off guard, not to mention shocked by their eldest child's claim, the parents for the moment were left speechless. This gave Meagan an opportunity to further speak her mind. Her surprising revelations came as though they were in a race with the storm's deadly potential. Bottled up emotions now spilled from the seventeen-year-old's lips. Holding nothing back, she blind-sided her parents with a heart wrenching truth-punch. Pulling from the past, Meagan revealed a conversation she overheard between her parents shortly after Bobby was diagnosed with cancer. One late night the two spoke on a back patio, and without their knowledge, Meagan had listened through an open window.

"I heard you say to Mom, if Bobby was to die, you had nothing to live for...and Mom, you agreed."

Of-course what she had heard, were words spoken out of desperation by grieving parents. Meagan's interpretation then and now, was that she didn't matter, and the way things were handled from that point on only validated her conclusion. She shared how the family changed in those days after the diagnosis, how nothing seemed to matter except Bobby.

As Meagan openly shared, the other stranded could have easily viewed her as a selfish teen. However, she was just a child herself when all of this took place. Just as her parents struggled with the possibility of losing their youngest, Meagan struggled with feelings over losing her parents. Not to mention, the responsibility of watching her sisters fell into the fourteen-year-old's lap.

Kelly tried to explain how it was a tough time for everyone. She wanted her daughter to know how much she appreciated her help.

Meagan interrupted her, "That's just it mother, I wasn't looking to be appreciated."

Her comment was impactful to say the least. It was followed up with a one-two punch that had both parent's reacting. Meagan revealed how she had secretly wished she too would have been diagnosed with cancer.

"Now that's a horrible thing to say, absolutely horrible," her father remarked.

"I know that now, but back then, I thought ..." At this point, Meagan's eyes began to glass over. Tears ran down the contours of her cheeks in black runny mascara lines.

"How could you even think that?" her mother said choking back tears.

Her parent's reactions made someone in the cabin very uncomfortable. Mr. Cartwright, raised his wooden staff into the air, motioning for the parents to stay back. He then proceeded to drag a chair over to where Meagan sat with her knees tucked up under her chin. Sitting directly in front of her, he now spoke only to the teen.

"Look....look into my eyes child," he said softly.

Her head slowly raised up and the normally defiant teen did just as he asked. Between the storm, and the fact that the two spoke in a whisper, the others could not hear their conversation. The parents became very uncomfortable with this situation. Here was a man they assumed was mentally unstable, now talking to their impressionable daughter in private. They longed to know what he could be saying to her. Twice, the parents tried to move in closer and each time Mr. Cartwright, hearing their footsteps, raised his wooden staff motioning them to stay back. Meagan never once looked away from his piercing white eyes nor made a single inference that she was scared. After more than twenty minutes of private conversation, the two rose up at the same time. He stood with his hands to his side while Meagan hugged his towering frame.

"Speak your truth child," he stated as he pulled away. He now motioned for the parents to come over, and in passing he told them, "keep your mouths shut, it's easier to hear that way."

Both mother and father sat down together in the chair across from their daughter. Her tears were now wiped in black smears across her cheeks. She again spoke to her parents, yet this time with an entirely different demeanor. Anger was now replaced by a softer side of the teen, something seldom seen by her parents. Meagan shared openly, and for the most part, uninterrupted.

Right away she let her parents know that she never hated either of them. Instead, it was what happened to the family that she hated.

"Cancer took more than just Bobby," she remarked.

"What do you mean?" her father asked.

Meagan did her best to answer her father's question in her own unique way, explaining first and foremost, how she felt cancer had taken her entire family. From the time of the diagnosis, both parents stopped attending her soccer games and eventually even stopped asking if her team had won or lost. She shared about a report card with straight 'A's' that hung on the refrigerator for weeks, without a single word of praise. Meagan soon learned that if she wanted attention, it would have to come from acting out. Negative attention, she discovered, was far better than no attention at all.

"I waited three weeks before I took the report card down," she stated.

"Honey, your brother was very sick," her father interjected, "we were just doing everything we could to keep him alive."

"I understand that now," she responded.

Meagan revealed how Mr. Cartwright explained things to her in a way that now made sense. Understanding, that one of toughest things a parent can face, is a sick child. The only thing harder, is to lose that child. No one can understand the pain, unless they have been through it, and no parent is ever prepared for that loss. Mr. Cartwright had told her this in a way that she could now understand. He himself had lost a son, and shared how his heart was still torn.

Meagan's father, also needing some clarity, had something that he needed to understand. He recalled how Meagan originally spent every waking moment caring for her brother, even giving up her weekends to be with him. This all changed when Bobby got too sick to be at home. Her father wanted to understand why she stopped talking to Bobby...why she stopped caring.

Meagan tried to answer him, her mouth opened and yet the words did not come. Tears on the other hand fell freely, but the words got lost somewhere between her mouth and her lips. Mr. Cartwright returned to the corner where the three sat together. He handed Meagan a red handkerchief and then spoke on her behalf.

"When someone we love is sick," Mr. Cartwright explained, "we make promises that are not in our power to keep."

He said this as he gently rubbed the gold band on his wedding ring finger. He then revealed that Meagan had made such a promise to her brother. What Mr. Cartwright had no way of knowing was that both parents had also made promises to Bobby, the kind they could not keep.

Understanding one another's guilt over broken promises brought mother, daughter and father together in a long overdue embrace. There were tears and apologies smothered in hugs. For both parents, it had been over two years since they had been this close to their daughter. Holding her brought great joy, while at the same time a painful reminder of how frail she had really become.

Mr. Cartwright was still standing above them, still rubbing the gold band on his wedding ring finger. After a few minutes, he tapped his wooden staff on the floor gaining the attention of all seven stranded. Amber and Makayla quickly joined the family with much needed hugs of their own. Mr. Cartwright, Landon and BC gave the family their privacy as best they could in such a small cabin.

After a few minutes, Dale broke away from his family and walked over to the strange, yet intriguing, cabin owner.

"You brought my family back together," Dale stated with gratitude. "For that, I owe you a thank you."

Mr. Cartwright placed a wad of tobacco between his cheek and gum before he spoke. In a very low tone so that only Dale could hear him, he stated, "You owe me nothing."

He then chewed on his tobacco while pointing his staff towards the other six. "Now them .... you owe, you owe them big time," he whispered.

"What do mean?" Dale asked rather confused.

"You and I both know what I mean."

CHAPTER 9: THE BEARDED MESSENGER

N THE LITTLE TOWNS to either side of the Siskyous, the news was spreading fast of two missing vehicles, presumed trapped on Devil's slide. Warden Ridge McCallister was already making the treacherous drive towards Pine Bluff. As a volunteer with the Morgansville search and rescue team, he felt he could be of some assistance. During the drive, he listened to local radio broadcasts. Most news commentators were holding out hope, while some were already assuming the worst.

Brave men and women, ready to head up the mountain, gathered at the foot of Devils Slide. Each one aware of the dangers that lay ahead once the gates were opened. No one knew the risks better than Commander Greg Jones. Sending his rescue teams up too soon could put their lives in danger, while on the other hand, waiting too long just might be the deciding factor between a rescue and a body recovery.

In a small window five thousand feet up, Landon stood looking out at a winter war zone. In his own private thoughts, he knew that there would be no rescue tonight. Even if attempts were to be made, both abandoned vehicles were now most likely buried in two feet of snow. It also didn't help that the seven were hidden away in a cabin beyond the tree line. If by chance a rescue attempt was to be made, they could easily pass right by the stranded.

Amber now joined Landon at the window, her small frame appearing even smaller next to his massive size. In a shaky little voice, she asked him if anyone was out there looking for them. He hesitated for a moment, then responded, "Yes, they're coming, we just need to be patient."

Landon chose to give hope to Amber, even when he knew perfectly well that anyone attempting a rescue in these conditions would just be putting their own life in jeopardy. That assumption was being validated by the storm now centered directly above. A dramatic shift in the winds had taken place. Where they had been punishing the sides of the structure, they now concurrently slammed straight down upon the roof line. Each gust came with a formidable challenge to the integrity of every cross beam and ceiling joist. One after another, after another, took aim on the little mountain top cabin at Unforgiven. A few gusts even found their way straight down the chimney, resulting in sparks spraying across the room's old woven rug. This happened multiple times. Landon and BC jumped into action, stomping out potential fire starting sparks. To the left, to the right, backwards and forwards they stomped. Both men bumped into one another like a couple of drunk cloggers at a fireside hoedown. Their actions could have been seen as humorous had it not been for the serious nature of the matter.

A continuous barrage of snow packed gusts followed, each a little less intense as the storm moved across the ridge. If the stranded thought for one second the worse was over, they would be dead wrong. In most cases, the tail end of a storm usually holds the biggest punch.

Again, a diversion was needed from the storm and this time it came well past the dinner hour. Queued by a growling stomach, Landon grabbed the gift basket of baked goods to share ... only ... there were no baked goods. Beneath the plastic wrap and tissue were an assortment of salt cured meats along with a variety of cheeses. The mayor's wife must have given up on baking. "Hallelujah," Landon shouted.

Grabbing an old porcelain plate off the shelf, he laid out the edibles, and then made the rounds. Everyone indulged, except for Meagan.

"No thanks I'm a vegetarian."

"Ah yes, the Indian word for bad hunter," Landon joked, "sorry to hear this".

"It's a choice," Meagan replied.

"Not a choice you'll ever see me making."

Interestingly though, when no one was looking, Meagan swiped a few slices of the cured meat and nibbled them down in secrecy. At this point, the vegetarian was now off the wagon. Everyone was enjoying the food until something very fowl filled the air. It didn't come from outside, it originated from within. Landon was not sure if the odor came from him. However, he graciously took the blame just the same.

"Sorry, I suffer from irritable bowel disease," he admitted.

Meagan, holding her nose asked, "Do you think maybe it's due to your diet?"

"Nope, no way," he replied.

"How do you know?"

"Because I'm not on a diet."

This round of questioning really didn't matter as there was someone in the room whose red face now matched her red hair.

It also happened to be where the foul odor was most intense. Amber was immediately asked by her parents to apologize, followed by an inquiry to the whereabouts of the bathroom. Mr. Cartwright opened the back door and pointed to a little outhouse underneath the eve. Amber's father stood just outside of the primitive one-seater, shining a flashlight over the half door. Mrs. Kenwood took this time to explain to the other three men that her daughter had not felt well ever since eating at Big Foot Burgers.

Just the mere mention of this roadside restaurant had Landon excited to report that he often ate there. In fact, he told the others how his name was embossed on the Big Foot Hall of Fame plaque. Just as he was about to reveal how he had achieved this honor, a loud high pitch scream came from out back. Kelly rushed to the open door just as Amber flew past still pulling up her pants. Embarrassed, she quickly threw herself beneath the bear skin on the sofa.

"What happened?" Kelly frantically asked her husband.

"I'm not sure. She said something grabbed her and wouldn't let go."

"What?"

"I don't know."

Mr. Cartwright interjected, thinking he was pretty sure as to what had happened. He explained how the outhouse toilet seat was made of metal. When it's wet and icy like tonight, things tend to stick to it, such as skin.

"You sat on a dirty old toilet seat?"

"Shut up Makayla," Amber yelled from beneath the bearskin.

Meagan stepped in to comfort her younger sister, something quite out of nature for her. This in return also brought out a rare gentle side of Makayla as well. Before long, all three sisters remarkably gathered together, cuddling beneath the bear skin.

Here it was Christmas Eve, no Christmas feast or Christmas tree, and yet the three youngest stranded had found a little of the holiday spirit.

Landon was back to looking out the window. He was well aware of how dire the whole situation had really become. Storms in the higher altitudes can often circle in place keeping the road closed for days at a time. Glancing over at the fireplace he noticed only three logs remained, hardly enough to even last through the night.

Meanwhile, Mr. Cartwright was busy placing two chairs next to a bench in the cabin's little nook. After moving an old rocker into the same area, he ordered the adults to come sit. Mr. Kenwood attempted to ask a question during this time but was abruptly interrupted.

"I ask the questions," Mr. Cartwright announced, "now sit."

As soon as everyone was seated, the strange old man placed his chair directly in front of Landon's, their knees touching one another's. His piercing white eyes stared directly ahead. Once again, Mr. Cartwright's sanity came into question.

"You, Mr. Landon Chase, tell us about your best childhood Christmas."

"I think I'll take a pass," Landon replied.

"There will be no passing," Mr. Cartwright informed him.

Landon leaned back in his chair and crossed his legs. He ran his fingers through his hair several times as if frustrated by the question. "I have only bad childhood Christmas memories," he stated.

Mr. Cartwright pointed towards the door, informing him that he could share or he could leave.

Landon waited a few seconds, as if maybe a third option was going to be offered. It wasn't. Reluctantly, he began to share how his mother ran off when he was only three, so he never had a Christmas memory that included her. As for his father, Christmas was just another reason to get drunk.

"So, I think I'll take that pass?" Landon again requested.

Mr. Cartwright responded with no words at first, instead his bushy eyebrows raised up in anger exposing even more of his piercing white eyes. He scooted his chair just a little closer and in a menacing voice said, "Please, do not anger me."

"Alright, you want Christmas, I got one for you!" Landon replied with an agitated tone. "I was twelve, no wait, I was eleven. It was the year I beat up Timmy Dutro for calling me a bean pole."

"Wait a minute," Kelly interrupted. "Someone actually called you bean pole?"

"Hey, when your father spends all the money on alcohol and cigarettes instead of food, you stay pretty lean," Landon remarked. "Anyway, there was this lady that lived in the same run-down trailer park as my father and me. Mrs. Bowman was her name. She was poor and I think she ate cat food at least that was the rumor."

As the story continued, the others listened as Landon shared how Mrs. Bowman invited him and some other children to go see Santa. Apparently, jolly old St. Nick was visiting the Griffin Hardware store that year. Landon remembered how he didn't ask for his father's permission. For one, he would have just said no, and besides, every Saturday his father would go to the town of Walton. He never knew why he went there, just that he did, and would be gone all day.

Seeing Santa was just something to do, as at eleven years old, Landon didn't believe. He wanted to, but his father had told him that he didn't exist. So, like all the other snot nosed kids that day, Landon shared how he had sat on Santa's lap and told him what he wanted, knowing full well he would never get it, or anything for that matter.

"Well there it is ... that's my Christmas memory," Landon remarked.

"Wait a minute, what did you ask Santa for?" Kelly questioned.

"I...I don't remember," he hesitantly replied. "I do remember though, each of us boys got these miniature rubber hammers."

"They gave hammers to kids?" Kelly asked.

"Well, it was a hardware store ma'am. I think the girls got something stupid like a doll. Anyway, that's my Christmas story."

Mr. Cartwright was still staring directly at Landon. He insinuated there was more to be told. "Finish the story," he demanded.

Landon informed his cabin host, as well as the others, that this Christmas story did not have a happy ending, so maybe it was now time for someone else to share.

"Finish–the story," Mr. Cartwright again demanded.

Again, rather reluctantly, Landon went on to share about that day. Apparently, one of the little rubber hammers had a green dot on the end of the handle. Whoever had this one would receive a special gift beneath a large box. As it turned out, Landon's hammer had that green dot. Everyone clapped and cheered as he went forward that day. When the box was raised up, a bright red bicycle was revealed. It was the coolest thing he had ever laid his eyes on, complete with a front headlight, handlebar streamers and two side mirrors ... and the best part, it was his ... all his. That night, he slept with it next to his bed, he told the others.

"Sounds like an ok Christmas to me," BC commented.

"Yeah, it was.....until that following morning."

At this point, Landon's whole disposition changed. His crossed leg dropped to the floor heavy and deliberate. He looked over at the three girls on the sofa as he considered whether his story was appropriate for young ears.

"They're asleep," Mr. Cartwright assured him. "I can hear their snores."

A chill ran down Landon's spine. How would a blind man know that he had looked in their direction and, furthermore, know the reason why...

"CONTINUE!" Mr. Cartwright gruffly demanded.

All adult eyes were now on Landon as he struggled on how to proceed. Rubbing his lips together as if he was angry, he finally spoke. "Okay, you want Christmas? Here's Christmas for you. I had one nice thing, one thing that was mine, and I wake up to find it's gone."

Kelly leaned forward in her chair and asked simply, "What happened?"

"What happened? That drunken no good father of mine took my bike, sold it, and bought his next three day binge."

"I don't know what to say," Kelly remarked, searching for just the right words. "I just want to cry... "

"You want to cry?" Landon asked. "Well I wasn't allowed to cry...but that morning, I did, just long enough to receive my old man's Christmas gift."

Landon paused just long enough to point out a two-inch scar above his left eye.

"Yep, he sold my bike, got drunk, and when I cried about it, I got an empty bottle to the head," he told the others. "Thank God for Mrs. Bowman though, she convinced my father I needed stitches. That's when I got to tell the doctor how it happened."

"... and what did the doctor do about it?" Mr. Kenwood asked.

"Nothing .... because I told the doctor exactly what my father told me to tell him."

"Which was, what?"

"My dad got me a new bike for Christmas, I fell off of it, hit my head, exactly what didn't happen."

"And how did that make you feel?" Mr. Cartwright inquired.

At this point, Landon was done with his walk down Christmas memory lane. He now turned the tables on his host, demanding to know.

"WHO ARE YOU? ... seriously, who do you think you are?"

"I am the man with the last three logs, so be careful."

"That's another thing," Landon quickly pointed out. "We have been here for six or seven hours now, and the same logs still burn. What are they, magic logs?"

"No ... just properly aged logs."

"Ok ...OK ...YOU WIN!" Landon said out of frustration. "So what is your game, your angle? What do you want from me?"

"I got what I wanted from you," Mr. Cartwright told him.

"And just what would that be?"

"For you to remember how it was with your father."

"You're crazy! I'm done talking to you!"

"Good! Now you can listen" Mr. Cartwright shot back.

The giant man now stood and leaned heavily upon his wooden staff. Unexpectedly, he told Landon how very sorry he was for his unfortunate childhood. He then changed the topic and began sharing about a little boy he once knew a very long time ago.

Apparently, much like Landon, this little boy was born unwanted by his father. As for his mother, she was young and naïve. After giving birth, she was beaten by her boyfriend, the father, as he blamed her for the pregnancy. At one point, she was pushed down a flight of stairs, breaking both legs and her hip. Young, scared, and feeling she had no other options, she deserted the father, as well as her baby boy. Mr. Cartwright seemed to struggle most when he explained why the father was not fit to raise a child. Mentally unstable, his psychotic episodes had him acting out in severely abusive ways. The young boy lived in constant fear, never knowing when his next unprovoked beating would come. At only fourteen years old, he ran away.

"A child on the run either ends up finding help, or more trouble," Mr. Cartwright said rather solemnly.

In this case, it was revealed that the young boy found himself in situations just as deplorable as those in which he had run from. Strangers abused him in ways that took his innocence and left his sole hollow. By sixteen the young man turned to alcohol and by seventeen he had a child out of wedlock.

At this point, Mr. Cartwright once again turned his attention to Landon. He asked in a rather sympathetic tone, "How do you feel about this young boy?"

"Well of course it angers me," Landon replied.

"And it should," Mr. Cartwright agreed. "This boy grew up never getting the help he needed, do you agree?"

"Not only do I agree. I think his father was no better than mine," Landon added.

"What if I told you this boy grew up to be just like your father?"

"I would say, why wouldn't he? Like you said, he never got the help he needed."

"You're right, Landon. He never got the help he needed, but is that a good enough excuse?"

"I see it as an explanation rather than an excuse" Landon fired back.

"So then, the fact that this boy grew up, had a child, and beat that child, you write it off as an explanation?" Mr. Cartwright questioned him.

"No, but no one ever helped him."

"What about him helping himself?"

Landon struggled on how to answer this question, or more precisely didn't have one to give. Mr. Cartwright returned to his seat in front of him. Once again he looked straight into Landon's eyes as he spoke to him. "That boy ... the one who was beaten by his father and never got help, his name was Leonard. He was your father, Landon ....."

Other than the storm's howls and the light crackle of the fire, the room went silent. If what Mr. Cartwright had shared was true, it was information Landon had never heard until now. All the abuse he had endured at the hands of his father now fell into a gray area, somewhere between unacceptable excuses and sad explanations. There was a tension in the air, as to how Landon would respond.

"How do you know this about my father?" Landon asked.

"I knew your grandfather," Mr. Cartwright responded vaguely.

"From where?"

"From his time at the Walton State Mental Hospital."

For the moment, Mr. Cartwright let everything sink in before he spoke again. He let Landon absorb the fact that he came from a family of abusive men. A father and grandfather that had explanations for why they committed such horrific acts of abuse. Yet, they were nothing more than sorry excuses. Where the grandfather had started the cycle of abuse, Leonard had only continued it. So the question arose, where did this leave Landon in the cycle? Had it really ended with him? Mr. Cartwright felt he had the answer.

Though Landon had never been abusive, he also had never raised a child. Yes, he had been married four times, but also divorced four times. Mr. Cartwright was aware of the real reason each marriage had failed, a truth that Landon had kept a secret. Somehow, a perfect stranger exposed what he had absolutely no way of knowing. The fact that Landon divorced each wife as each had expressed interest in wanting to have a child. The cycle of abuse had not really ended, as much as it had been avoided.

"Time to stop running," Mr. Cartwright told him.

This inevitably angered and baffled Landon at the same time. How could this stranger know his truths, and why was he pressing him so hard. Just as Landon was about to ask for an answer to both questions, Mr. Cartwright exposed one more thing.

"You have a son who needs you," the bearded messenger stated.

This revelation had Landon rising to feet. He slowly made his way over to the cabins small window. With his back to the other four adults, he responded to this shocking allegation.

"Yes, I ran from each of my marriages," he admitted. "I ran from the thought of having another child... but I never ran from my son."

Turning to face the other four adults, he again confirmed that everything presented by Mr. Cartwright was true. He was in-fact a runner, running from his past and even from the prospect of fatherhood. As for his one and only son, Landon insisted he did the right thing.

"I gave him a chance to have what I never had, a real family."

CHAPTER 10: THE BEARDED MESSENGER (PART II)

I N THE DRIVEWAY OF Bill and Betty Applegate's home, the old Cadillac was chained up and ready to roll. Grandpa loaded the back with blankets, rope, and an old snow shovel he had quickly repaired with a roll of duct tape. This very well could be the only rescue ever initiated in a hearse. Kissing his teary-eyed wife at the door, he promised he would return with the kids in time for Christmas morning pancakes.

Once out of the driveway, Grandpa was able to allow his tears to build and fall. Up until now, he had stayed strong for the sake of his wife. There was a real battle going on between his heart and mind. One generated a driving force of hope, while the other a realistic preparation for the possible outcome. After serving forty-five years with the Carmody County Highway Patrol, retired Major Bill Applegate was well aware of the odds in favor of a negative (or you could say "the odds against a positive") outcome.

Inside the cabin at Unforgiven, Landon had now returned to his seat next to the other four adults. He had just confirmed that at age seventeen, he had deserted his newborn son. Over the last ninety minutes, Mr. Cartwright had pushed, prodded and pulled information out of him, and now it was Landon himself who freely chose to expose more of his past.

It was true that Leonard was his father and, like most parental figures, he had a huge impact on his son's life, though not in many positive ways. Almost everything about his father, Landon tried not to emulate. Unfortunately, 'the abused' have the propensity to become an abuser. That potential cycle can be stopped if appropriate counseling is pursued. By learning about his father's upbringing, it provided at least some form of understanding.

With most of the skeletons out of his closet, Landon himself felt the need to rattle a few bones. Mainly he wanted to address the reason he had abandoned his son. In doing this, he chose to go all the way back to the day he ran from his father and how he ended up in a town less than twenty miles away. That's where he met a young girl by the name of Jessica. She sat across the table from Landon at the Koch County Library. She was studying; he was perusing the employment section of the local newspaper. Neither could keep their eyes off the other. Homework and job searching were soon put on hold that day. Instead, a four-hour conversation in the nearby park took place. Side by side on a swing-set, the two opened up to one another. Casual conversation eventually gave way to much deeper topics. The two soon discovered that although they were from two different social classes, they both had similar dark secrets hidden away in their separate worlds. Abuse has no boundaries. It can happen in any home, from an old trailer on an Indian reservation where Landon grew up, to a gated estate where Jessica lived with her parents.

Their relationship got serious almost right way. Jessica would sneak food in her book bag and the two would rendez-vous wherever they could without being seen. As for lodging, Landon found a way to avoid spending what little money he made doing odd jobs. Every night, just before 6 pm, he would hide behind a bush by the back door of the Callan's Furniture Store. When the owner would take out the garbage just before closing, Landon would slip in unnoticed. His routine was to first hide beneath a desk. Once old man Callan was gone, he would bathe from a sink before bedding down in one of the king size display beds.

Eventually Jessica's parents found out about the relation-ship, putting an abrupt end to their time together. Landon was not suitable for their daughter, at least not in their eyes. They were white and wealthy; he was poor and Native American. Hiding his heritage was not something he was brought up to do, but at the same time his father made no efforts to embrace their culture. Young and in love, Landon would do just about anything for Jessica, including making every effort to gain her parents' respect. The fact that they objected to him being Native American was something he was incapable of changing.....and yet, he naively tried.

Walking by a newspaper box, Landon noticed the heading on the front page of the Koch County Tribune. Across the top of the page in big bold print, the headline read, 'Most Respected Man in politics'. Just beneath the headline was a picture of Southern Oregon's congressman, Daryl Capurro. Landon quickly paid the ten cents for the Tribune. With the paper in hand, he ran to the local barber shop where he planned to get the same hairstyle as the congressman. Upon entering the barber shop that day, he asked one of the men inside for a haircut.

The elderly owner took one look at Landon's jet-black braided ponytail and remarked, "We don't serve your kind here."

Racism was something he had not encountered back on the reservation. Walking away from the barber shop that day, he felt angry and hurt at the same time. About a half block away, someone grabbed ahold of his shoulder. When he turned around he discovered it was one of the men from the barber shop, a large white man with a big bushy beard and tobacco stained teeth. His grip was strong and his voice was deep and scratchy.

"Every bucket of apples has a few rotten ones," he remarked to him that day.

This made no sense to Landon at the time. However, he figured it must have been meant in a nice way, as the man smiled afterwards.

"Go on over to Clyde's on 4th street, he'll cut your hair," he said pointing down past the railroad tracks.

At first, Clyde the barber, was reluctant to cut Landon's pony tail off, not because he was racist, but for exactly the opposite reason. When Clyde learned that he was doing it gain the respect of his girlfriend's parents, he questioned if it would really change their views. "Trying to hide your heritage is a lot like trying to hide your shadow on a sunny day," he told Landon. Eventually, the African-American barber fulfilled his seventeen-year-old customer's request, but not without dispensing some last words of wisdom.

"You can put white paint on a grizzly, but that don't make him no polar bear," Clyde had said while snipping off the 12-inch pony tail.

Before leaving, Landon asked where he might be able to purchase an inexpensive shirt and tie. Clyde directed him down the street to the Southern Baptist Gospel Mission. "Ask for Deacon Roe," he told him. "He'll fix you up."

Not only did Roe outfit him that day with a shirt and tie, but also with a pair of slightly worn wingtip shoes and a hounds tooth sport coat. The only thing left now was for Landon to find a respectable full-time job, which he did at Mondon Memorial Hospital.

Landon told his fellow stranded how his faith in others was both questioned and reinforced in that same day. As for himself, he remembered how proud he felt when he placed that hospital clearance badge upon his chest. It was now time to reintroduce himself to Jessica's parents.

Even with his full-time janitorial job, professional attire and new clean-cut appearance, Jessica's parents did not budge from their previous racist stance. Landon was warned this time, at gun point, to stay away, and as for Jessica, she was forced to obey. Months went by without the two seeing each other. Then one night, Jessica was admitted into Mondon Memorial hospital. She arrived with a black eye, a bruised cheek ... and eight months pregnant.

Landon's boss, Dylan James, was a kind elderly man who sympathized with their situation, even going as far as to help orchestrate a few secretive visits, during which time the two talked about their future and, of course, their baby. On the fourth day, Landon walked past her room just as he had done the previous three. When he glanced in, he saw that she was gone and the hospital bed was neatly made. His heart shuddered as he frantically ran down the hospital's hall. Dylan James, seeing him, grabbed his arm and led him to a small janitor's closet. He quickly settled Landon down, having him sit on an upturned mop bucket. That's when he informed him that Jessica had gone into premature labor.

Landon recalled how he jumped up and shouted, "Where, where is she, is it a boy or a girl?"

With both hands, Dylan James shoved him back down on bucket. He told him to calm down before they both got into trouble. In a soft voice he then told Landon that Jessica's parents and his baby were on the 2nd floor.

"It's a boy," he remarked rather solemnly.

As Landon recalled, his boss then turned and placed his hand on the door knob. He stood there for a few seconds with his back to Landon saying nothing. He then opened the door to leave, but not before telling him that Jessica died giving birth.

Not knowing what else to say, he slipped out the door with a simple, "I'm sorry."

Landon remained in the small janitor's closet for a better part of an hour. His heart fighting with his emotions and his mind wrestling with some important decisions. In a cruel twist of fate, the only person he ever loved had died giving birth to the only person who needed his love.

As the other four listened intently, Landon did his best to explain what went through his seventeen-year old mind that day. He knew absolutely nothing about raising a child, especially on his own. All the happiness of the gift of a child was ripped away with the loss of Jessica. What possibly could a broken-hearted boy give to a child who needed a Mom and a Dad.

Tears were already falling down Kelly's face. She could only imagine how hard it must have been for Landon that day. Here he was, with no family that could help, and the toughest decision he would ever have to make.

When it came right down to it, Landon had only one person he could think of to turn to, his father. It had been nine months since he had last seen him, and as it would turn out, that would remain the last time. Leonard had passed away four months earlier, unbeknownst to Landon. While sitting on Mrs. Bowman's trailer step, he learned how his father had tried to sober up after he left. A lifetime of alcohol abuse and the withdrawals from quitting ended up killing him. Mrs. Bowman chose to put it this way; Leonard died trying to become a better person, and with the hopes of becoming a better father. His efforts were sadly unrealized. The decision on what to do about his newborn son was left to Landon alone. His decision was one that he regretted from the very second he had made it.

"I ran," Landon shared remorsefully. "I thought my son should have more than I alone could give."

"That must have been a very sad time for you," Kelly interjected.

"It still is," he remarked. "I guess I could have easily become an alcoholic just like Leonard... but fortunately I chose food instead."

"Do you know if your son was ever adopted?" Mr. Cartwright asked.

"I don't," Landon replied. "I just know that Jessica's parents tried, but were denied."

"Tell us why," Mr. Cartwright demanded.

"All I know is someone at the hospital reported Mr. Canton's abuse of Jessica."

"Who told you that?"

"I believe it was Mrs. Bowman who told me," Landon replied. "Why do you ask?"

Mr. Cartwright did not answer and, instead, took a seat. BC, however, had a question for Landon. He asked for his son's birthdate.

"November 26th, 1992," Landon replied.

This answer had BC popping up out of his chair and grabbing for his duffle bag. Ripping it open, his red leather-bound Bible, the gift from Grandma, fell into Kelly's lap. He was so anxious to get to something else that, for the moment, he did not retrieve the Bible.

"Here, here it is," he announced in excitement.

In his hand he now had a small box, the one that Warden Ridge McCalister had given to him. Earlier, when Landon had stopped for gas in Pine Bluff, BC had opened his gift. He now only had to lift the lid to pull out the contents, a single piece of paper. To the others it looked like some sort of legal document.

"Thanksgiving!" BC blurted out. "Your son was born on Thanksgiving day ..."

Landon answered with just a nod yes.

"...and Jessica, her last name was Canton ...not Smith?"

"I never said it was Smith," Landon replied rather confused.

"Unbelievable," BC proclaimed, shaking the paper in his hand. "Canton isn't my middle name...it's my last name ..."

"What exactly are you trying to say," Landon asked as he rose forward in his seat.

"I'm not trying to say anything, I'm telling you ....my mother was Jessica Canton".

"WHAT!"

"LOOK!" BC replied handing over his birth certificate.

While Landon looked it over, BC explained how his old birth certificate had gotten lost. Warden McCallister had promised he would order a new one, which he did, only he somehow received a copy of the original ... and not the one provided to the adoption agency.

"If you look at this birth certificate, you will see that my name is not Billy Canton Smith. It's actually Billy Smith Canton. And look, look right here," BC stated as he pointed to the line that listed his mother's name, "Jessica Lindsay Canton."

"That would mean...," Landon started to say as BC finished it for him, "... you're my father."

Both studied the document together and then at first only shook hands. As the shock wore off and the reality sank in, the handshaking turned to hair ruffling, back smacking and eventually a long awaited hug. When they finally stepped back from one another, they looked at each other for the very first time as father and son. So many similarities missed were now as plain as day, from the same jet-black hair and broad nose to the almost identical cheek bone structure.

Landon joked, "If I lost ten pounds, we would practically be twins."

"That's funny," BC responded. "I was thinking the same thing, only if I gained a hundred pounds."

Father and son once again embraced, laughing while each tried to hide their tears. Kelly, on the other hand, was already on to her third tissue. As for Mr. Cartwright, his eyes seemed just a little less piercing. Mr. Kenwood, however, seemed to react very strangely to the whole father–son reunion. It was obvious to Kelly that something was wrong. He seemed agitated, even angry …but why …

CHAPTER 11: THE PUZZLE

ON THE OREGON SIDE of the mountain, both men and women had now gathered at the designated staging area. Snowplows and other rescue vehicles idled in place filling the air with a haze of diesel smoke. Commander Greg Jones was currently speaking with Ridge McCallister, who had just arrived offering his help. Their conversation was cut short by a red Cadillac hearse that came sliding to a stop in front of them. Greg was quite shocked to see that the driver was, in fact, his old boss from twenty years back. These two men neither liked nor respected one another. The fact that the gate was still locked certainly didn't sit well with retired officer Bill Applegate. The last thing he expected to see was a group of rescuers standing around while lives hung in the balance.

"I'm confused, is this a search party or Christmas party," Bill yelled as he exited the Cadillac.

Commander Jones instantly defended his position of not sending anyone up Devil's Slide.

"It's too dangerous up there," he firmly stated.

"For you, I'm sure it is," Applegate said loud enough for all to hear. "I'm talking to the real men and women ...now let's get up there."

Commander Jones was not going to risk lives to save lives, a point of view completely opposite from that of his old boss. Applegate believed that taking risks resulted in rescues, and not recoveries. Stepping out in front of a snow plow's headlights, he proceeded to rip off his right glove exposing three missing fingers.

"Lost these to frost bite back in the winter of '82'," he told the others.

Applegate then shared how he and Greg's father, Jeff Jones, searched for a missing car during a blizzard. They spent two hours in waist deep snow, but eventually found the car resulting in four lives being saved.

"...now, let's get up there!"

"No, I won't allow it," Commander Jones replied.

Of course, this angered Applegate immensely, and he made it known. "If you want to sit around and sip your coffee, go ahead, but open that damn gate".

'The gate will open when I say it opens," Jones shot back.

"You're nothing like your father ... Jeff would've been up there and back already."

"My father died up on Devil's Slide doing one of your reckless rescues," the Commander reminded him.

"He died a hero," Applegate fired back, "something you never have to worry about. Now open the damn gate!"

"Listen old man, you better hop back in that hearse of yours and get the hell out of my sight."

This comment had Applegate taking several steps towards Greg. As he did so, he warned that if he didn't open the gate, he might end up laid out in the back of the Cadillac.

Ridge McCallister could see that this conversation was going nowhere positive. He walked past the eighty-seven year old, leaned in and whispered, "Follow me, I have a plan."

This of course caught Applegate's interest. He followed McCallister, but not before pulling a role of duct tape from his pocket and tossing it in Greg's direction. "Here, go fix that broken spine of yours."

It was a good thing that the well-respected warden had stepped in before things got any worse. As the two walked and talked, they learned about each other's relations with those stranded on the mountain. Once they reached McCallister's truck, they were joined by another individual. In the warmth of the cab, Jan Moncado from the Rogue River Search and Rescue, was introduced. She and McCallister agreed with Applegate, standing around was not going to save lives. They had a plan and the means to make it happen. Moncado was in charge of a four passenger snow cat idling in the staging area. Not only was this the only type vehicle that could handle the terrain above without a snow plow escort, but it was also equipped with every rescue apparatus imaginable. The plan was simple, all three would load into the snow cat and drive over to Crow Canyon Lake Road. From there, they would shoot across Susie's Meadow and enter Devil's Slide about 300-feet on the other side of the locked gate.

Less than ten minutes after their plan was devised, the three were tracking straight up Devil's Slide. Commander Greg Jones could not stop them, nor did he send anyone after them. However, what he did do was order Sgt. Rich Youngman to have Applegate's car towed. The request was something Youngman was not prepared to do, at least not at that exact moment. Walking up from behind Greg was Betty Applegate alongside two local celebrities, log tossing champions Bess and

Bertha Bogner. Everyone noticed the three ladies, except for Jones, who again ordered to have the Cadillac towed.

"You so much as touch my husband's car, my friends here will personally duct tape you to the front of a snowplow ... now ... would you be so kind as to open that gate".

Saving face, Greg announced that he was just about to order the gate to be opened. Within minutes, four snow plows fell into line, giving the earlier three gate crashers only a small lead. At a max speed of twenty miles per hour, Moncado's Bombardier snow cat howled as it made the climb upward. Three sets of eyes searched for any signs of the missing vehicles. They were prepared to go all the way up and down the other side if need be. Applegate watched to the right, McCallister to the left, and as for Moncado, she drove with her eyes on the thin white path ahead. The guardrails were merely fluffy white speed bumps that separated the road from the sheer cliffs of Devil's Slide.

At the top of the summit, inside the cabin at Unforgiven, Kelly was congratulating both men in regards to their fortunate reunification. After embracing BC, she handed him back his red leather-bound Bible. Putting it back in his duffle bag, he casually mentioned that it was a gift from Grandma C.

"Not my real grandmother," he told the others, "just a very good friend."

"Where did you meet her?" Landon asked out of curiosity.

His question confused the former inmate for obvious reasons. For one, Landon worked the Sunday shift on 'B Block', where he was housed. Secondly, the only way to enter BC's corridor was through the gate that Landon guarded.

"You know, the elderly lady who visited me every Sunday," BC reminded him.

"Who?"

"Grandma, with the pink cane ...!"

Landon had absolutely no idea who he was talking about. During BC's two years at Tunnel Creek, not one person ever logged in for visitation with the young man.

"You had no visitors," Landon confirmed.

"That's funny, because every Sunday she was in my cell."

"That's another thing." Landon added. "Visitations only take place in the visitation room, not in individual cells."

"Then explain this!"

Reaching into his duffel bag, BC pulled his Bible back out and handed it over to Landon. He asked him to read the personal note written on the inside cover.

"Alright, let's see what this will prove," Landon said as he flipped the Bible open. "Dearest William," he read, "may you always have hope where there is hopelessness and forgiveness when things seem unforgivable ... Love Grandma."

"Ok, now read the date underneath her name," BC directed.

"There is no date," Landon replied.

"What? Give me that."

Looking at it for himself, he found that Landon was right, there was no date. How could this possibly be, BC thought silently to himself. After all, he was certain that when he received the Bible, yesterday's date was beneath her name. Looking at it now for the second time, he witnessed that not only was there no date, but the writing was somewhat faded from age. His mind questioned his sanity, while his heart opened to the possibility of a miracle.

While father and son tried to figure things out, Kelly turned her attention towards her husband. She knew for certain he was uncomfortable with the discovery that BC was a former prisoner. However, that didn't explain his strange demeanor. He seemed agitated, possibly even angry. Before she had a chance to pull him aside for a private conversation, Mr. Cartwright was back to acting mentally unstable. Instead of using the last three logs sparingly, he tossed them into the fire all at once. The flames engulfed the dry wood with a loud whooshing sound.

"Why would you do that?" BC asked in bewilderment. "Are you crazy?"

"I don't know, maybe. Define crazy."

"Look in a mirror," Dale mumbled under his breath.

"Is that a blind joke?" Mr. Cartwright asked.

"No, not at all," Dale defended himself.

"Good, because that was about as funny as you driving under the influence."

"What are you talking about?"

"I'm talking about you falling asleep at the wheel."

Before this argument went any further, Landon interrupted stating, "Leave it be, it was an accident, case closed."

"OBJECTION!" Mr. Cartwright said in a raised voice. "You don't have all the facts, Counselor Chase. ...cause and affect ...we know the accident was the effect ... but what was the cause Counselor?"

"Not important," Landon shot back.

"Well now, who died and made you judge and jury?" Mr. Cartwright remarked as he made his way towards the front door. Reaching into the chest pocket of a coat that hung on one of the hooks, he pulled out a small cylinder prescription bottle.

"Exhibit one," Cartwright announced as he shook the bottle. "Oh my, sounds like you're almost out ..... time for a refill."

"Put them back," Dale demanded.

"What exactly am I putting back?" Cartwright asked as he popped several pills into his mouth.

"Aspirin, now put them back."

"Interesting ...because I have spent most of my adult life swallowing down every pharmaceutical known to mankind, and these feel and taste like ...oh yeah, most definitely, these are oxycodone. Good stuff by the way.....unless you're planning on driving a car. That would just be reckless, don't you think?"

"You're crazy," Dale uttered.

"How's this for crazy, I pop the last five pills in my mouth ...or..... What's behind door number two?...why it's the TRUTH."

Kelly and Landon noticed Dale's face was overcome with a look of shame.

"Okay, you made your point," Landon remarked.

"Did I counselor Chase, Did I really... because I think your pill popping friend here is taking something a little stronger than aspirin. WOW! Oh yeah, these are a lot stronger!"

"Enough with the dramatics," Landon remarked.

"Agreed," Cartwright shot back. "It's time for apologies, you know, like sorry I almost killed everyone on Christmas Eve, those kind of apologies."

"You're a little over the top," BC remarked.

"Over the top...hmm, that's better than six feet under, wouldn't you say?"

"STOP!" Dale yelled out. .... "Just stop."

With his head hung low and face flushed with shame, Dale now spoke with a tremor in his voice, "What he said is true ...all of it. ... he's right too, I owe everyone an apology."

The cabin at Unforgiven went silent, except for the faint snores of the three sleeping teens. Slowing rising to his feet, an ashamed Dale Kenwood made no excuses. He owned up to everything; falling asleep, taking the pills, and the fact that the pills were not aspirin as he first had stated, even going as far as to admit he had an addiction. For Kelly, this information was all shocking and new. Before this, she had no idea what had caused the accident. Her husband, the father of their children, had put everyone's life at risk. She had every reason to feel deceived and angry. In terms of an apology, Dale felt his actions were so far beyond a simple utterance of sorry. Forgiveness for what he had done was something he neither expected nor could imagine, and yet he underestimated his fellow man. Landon, following his son's lead, enacted the purest form of forgiveness of all. Both men forgave, without even being asked for forgiveness.

After the three men made amends, they hugged like most men do, smacking each other's backs, then quickly pulling away. It was now time for Dale to turn his attention to his wife. Kneeling down in front of her chair, he placed his hands gently upon hers. With no expectation of receiving forgiveness, he openly shared his truths, including acknowledging his actions of today and those of the last two years. While his wife had made progress in dealing with Bobby's passing, Dale had made absolutely no effort in the healing process. Pill after pill, he avoided facing reality; therefore, stagnating in self-pity and anger. His heart was held captive by hate for the man he held responsible for his son's death. Meanwhile, one daughter hid in her fantasy world, while another literally starved herself for attention.

"I hope one day you can forgive me," Dale said in a voice tainted with doubt.

Kelly had a choice. She could forgive, or like her husband, withhold it and let it destroy them both. For a brief moment, she reflected back to the Survivor's class she had taken shortly after Bobby's passing. There was an elderly lady that attended the same meetings. Like Kelly, she had lost a child. She never shared what had happened between her husband and their son, only that there were problems. Fortunately, just before his unexpected passing, he was able to forgive his father for everything.

Something the elderly lady had said to her back then, now echoed within her soul. A peacefulness came over Kelly as she whispered these same words in her husband's ear, "Forgiveness is as much for the forgiver as it is for the forgiven."

She then squeezed his hand, and in her own words whispered, "I forgive you."

The two embraced, followed by a tearful kiss.

It was now Dale who whispered in his wife's ear, telling her that he had something he needed to address, something that was long overdue.

Rising to his feet, Dale walked over to the cabin's little window. He turned and faced the other four. His eyes were focused solely on one person, and that person he addressed by his given name.

"Billy why were you at Tunnel Creek?" he asked

There was a period of a few seconds where nothing was said by the former inmate. He wasn't avoiding the question, just struggling with exactly how to reply. Finally, a three word answer came out of his mouth.

"Involuntary man slaughter," he replied.

"Were you guilty of that crime?" Dale asked.

"I was convicted."

"I didn't ask if you were convicted. I asked if you were guilty of that crime."

Billy answered the question while at the same time avoiding his own personal opinion.

"I was involved in an accident, one that I caused."

"So it was an accident ...," Dale probed.

"Well yes, but it was my fault."

"How was it your fault?"

Billy looked over at the cylindrical pill bottle that was still in Mr. Cartwright's hand. In no way was he attempting to compare his accident with that of the one Dale had caused earlier. However, the story was much the same.

"I was taking medication at the time that affected my judgment," he replied.

"Just like me then."

There was a slight hesitation before BC responded, "Only in my case someone actually died."

His answer came as Kelly rose up out of her chair. She made her way over to the window, quite certain she had come to the same conclusion as her husband. Like a puzzle, all of the pieces had fallen into place, except for one crucial piece, the one that brings the whole picture together.

Two years ago, Mr. Kenwood had taken their son Bobby to the Snow Park. There were designated boundary lines between where the children could play and the trail used by snowmobiles. For just one second, Dale took his eyes off his son to take a phone call. For whatever reason, Bobby crossed over that boundary, right into the path of a snowmobiler. The man who had hit him was injured and later arrested. The Kenwoods never even knew his full name, just that his first name was Billy. As for what he looked like, his helmet had never been removed that day, fearing a neck injury.

With his wife now by his side, both looked directly at the man they now believed was the driver of the snowmobile.

"How did your accident happen? Dale calmly asked.

"I guess I was driving too fast or, like I said before, my judgment was off."

"And what happened?"

"I hit a little boy with my snowmobile ... and that's all I remember. I was knocked unconscious".

And just like that, the last piece of the puzzle was placed in, and like all puzzles, they never quite look like the picture on the box. They are, after all, a mosaic of broken little pieces. In life, most of us encounter something that breaks us; maybe its abuse, or addiction, or maybe an accident that we caused. It is only through healing and/or forgiveness that we can become whole again. And just like the puzzle, our lives can be put back together, forming beautiful mosaics of our past brokenness.

For Billy, there was obvious pain in his voice as he explained how he felt about the accident. He shared how it had haunted him most days and even nights within his dreams. It was clear he felt the accident was solely his fault. What he did not know was that someone else felt the same guilt. The fact was, Dale's anger at the man on the snowmobile was in-part, misplaced. It was easier for him to blame Billy, than to turn the mirror upon himself. It was now time to be truthful ... it was time to forgive.

Very delicately, Dale shared that it was their son, Bobby, who ran out in front of his snowmobile that day. He went on to reveal that had he not taken a phone call, the tragic accident might never have happened.

After two years of Billy longing for the opportunity to apologize and hoping for forgiveness, the opportunity was now here. Only it was Dale who apologized, and it was Dale asking for Billy's forgiveness.

"Forgive you?" Billy spoke tearfully, "I should be asking you and your family to forgive me."

Both went back and forth on who should forgive who, until Landon interrupted them.

"How about you both forgive one another."

This suggestion was taken to heart and, thus, the unimaginable was imagined. Forgiveness blessed both the forgiver and the forgiven.

"It's like a miracle," Kelly remarked.

"Exactly," Mr. Cartwright agreed, "and it's what Bobby wanted."

"What do you mean it was what Bobby wanted?" Dale asked.

The bearded messenger stood before the others and smiled a tobacco stained smile. He turned his head and spit into the pill bottle that he still had in his possession.

"Bobby did his part. Now what are you all going to make of this?"

"Who are you?" Kelly asked. "Are you an angel?"

Mr. Cartwright laughed until he choked on his tobacco. "Do I look like an angel?" he sputtered.

CHAPTER 12: THE OLD ROCK CHIMNEY

ITH SO MUCH GOING on within the cabin at Unforgiven, the five adults had not noticed what had taken place outside. All of the storm's destructiveness had moved on, leaving a peaceful falling snow in its wake. Time had also passed, touching into a new day, that being Christmas. The bearded messenger faded into the background, giving the other four adults a chance to get better acquainted. It was at this point that the rubber banded bundle of letters was handed over to the intended recipients.

There was no time to dwell on the past. All four were now focused on today, tomorrow and the day after that. Dale and Kelly were thinking big ...ambitiously big. Their neighbor back home just so happened to be Dr. Alfred Oettle, President of the Brent Brooks School of Medicine.

"Where do you plan to finish your schooling?" Dale asked Billy.

"I have no idea," he replied. "For now, I am headed to the Cascade River Ranch."

"That sounds more like a veterinary school than a medical school."

Billy laughed as he explained that it was a not a school. It was, rather, his only option as a newly released inmate. Dale responded, "Not anymore!"

After making this off the cuff statement, Dale asked if he and wife might have a moment alone. In a cabin of this size, that simply meant going to the opposite corner. All three men made their way to the little nook.

As they stood there, Landon took notice of an old black and white framed photograph of a young girl on the wall. He inquired about her identity. When Mr. Cartwright referred to her as the most beautiful girl he had ever laid his eyes upon, it became evident that he had not always been blind. For Billy and Landon, it was also apparent that she was someone very special to him.

"I built this cabin for the two of us," Mr. Cartwright revealed. "It was a dream ...... and then the war changed everything."

Father and son both listened as the strange man slowly became a little less strange, and a little more understood. Mr. Cartwright began reminiscing about the war, recalling the day he made a very special promise, the kind of promise that men heading off to battle often made to their girlfriends. For nine months, he fought the enemy, followed by twelve more as a prisoner fighting to stay alive. He eventually returned home, but not the same man as when he left. Over seven thousand miles from the battle field and each day he awoke as if he was still there, still under his capturer's torment.

As he explained more about his mental state upon returning home, it became clear that his promise of marriage was a promise he was incapable of keeping. Soldiers with physical injuries were cared for, and yet those with mental disorders were more often than not, left to deal on their own. Many times these men ended up committing suicide, or like Mr. Cartwright, they became outwardly abusive. His anger and rage was out of control. He openly admitted that the mother of his child had no choice but to run from his abuse.

It took brave men to go to battle, but it also took equally brave women to fight for these men once they returned home. Wives, mothers and girlfriends fought for the returning soldiers they loved. They wanted nothing less than proper treatment for their mental disorders. The mother of Mr. Cartwright's son was one of these women. She demanded treatment for every soldier, especially for the one she never stopped loving. After over thirty years of seeking proper care for these men with wounded minds, as she called it, her plea finally reached the desk of the President. With his signature, a bill was passed and lives were changed. Treating the symptoms with just medications came to an end. Skilled counseling that got to the core issues that haunted these soldiers was introduced. Mr. Cartwright was one of these men that finally received proper care and all because of one woman...... a woman who never gave up ...and never stopped loving her man.

Mr. Cartwright shared with Billy and Landon how his recovery brought his family back together. It took time, but eventually his son came to him with forgiveness. As for the women who never stopped fighting for him, she too forgave. Forty five years after a promise of marriage was made, the two were married.

"Is your wife still alive?" Billy asked curiously.

"No, she died in a fire two years ago."

Just as father and son were giving their condolences, Dale asked for the three men to return. Both of the Kenwoods were claiming to have some amazing news. Kelly grabbed one of Billy's hands as Dale spoke on their behalf.

"You're going to medical school," he stated, looking directly at Billy.

"What ...where?"

"Brent Brooks Medical School in Los Angeles," Dale replied.

"...but how? I have no money, nowhere to live ......everything I own is in this duffle bag ..."

"We already thought of that," Dale responded. "Money is not a problem.....and it makes perfect sense for you to live with us."

Billy was totally and utterly speechless, so his father replied on his behalf.

"Makayla told me that you live in a gated community, is that true?" Landon asked.

"Yes," Dale replied.

"Great, my son accepts. After all, these last two years he's grown accustomed to living in a gated community."

At first only Landon laughed at his comment, but once Billy joined in, so did the others. Mr. Cartwright actually laughed the loudest, pounding his staff upon the floor at the same time. This in return, woke all three of the teens. After wiping their eyes and adjusting their clothing, they each took turns hugging their parents.

"I'm hungry!" Meagan blurted out.

Landon grabbed a package of beef jerky from his duffel bag and handed it over to Meagan. "Its beef .... but I believe the cow was a vegetarian." Meagan ate all but the last piece, which she offered back to Landon.

"No thanks, you have it," he replied. "I'm on a new diet."

A ray of light from the rising sun shined through the cabin's frosted window and across the floor. Christmas morning had come with the passing of the storm. The worst was certainly over ...or was it.

A worried look came over Mr. Cartwright. He could hear the main support beam of the old cabin snapping and cracking under the weight of the snow. The warmth of the sun did not help matters. The snow pack on the three large pine trees outside the front door were now falling like weighted powdery bombs. They landed upon the roof with a thud, causing the beam to crack and pop each time. Mr. Cartwright quickly had everyone gather their things and get out. He told them to seek shelter outside. Those that questioned his hasty concern were soon convinced of the urgency. With a punishing direct hit to the chimney, the entire rock structure crumbled down within the cabin's interior.

Burning logs rolled across the floor igniting everything they touched. The Kenwoods frantically grabbed what they could and made their way out. Mr. Cartwright yelled at the other two men to follow. Billy grabbed his duffle bag, but accidentally spilled the contents. His red leather bound Bible slid across the floor. In a matter of seconds it was engulfed in the flames. Again Mr. Cartwright yelled, "GET OUT NOW!"

Just beyond the three large pines, the seven gathered together. The cabin at Unforgiven creaked and moaned like an old wooded ship tossed in rough seas. There was no sign of Mr. Cartwright anywhere. They watched in horror as the entire rock and wood structure collapsed inward. Before long, the last burning board fell into a slushy white grave. It was as if the cabin at Unforgiven had never existed and as for Mr. Cartwright, he was nowhere to be found. Survival for the remaining seven now depended on one thing, and one thing only, the timing of their rescue. It was bitter cold and they had no food or shelter, so timing was everything.

Meagan alone cried out for Mr. Cartwright. Her voice pierced the winter chill, yet received no reply. Mourning his loss would have to wait, as every bit of strength would be needed to survive. In one last attempt, Meagan yelled out for the old bearded man. As her voice echoed across the snow-covered landscape, it was met by a rumbling sound of an engine. Landon knew very well what it was and shouted out, "We need to get to the road ... NOW!"

For the time being, all luggage would be left to be retrieved later. Moving fast was essential, while at the same time impossible. Every step in the newly laid snow had the stranded sinking waist deep, and in Amber's case almost to her shoulders. The trek was slow and tedious. For the teens, the pace was too fast. A decision was made for Billy and Landon to forge ahead of the Kenwoods, it was crucial that at least one of the stranded reach the road before the vehicle passed. It didn't take long for the two men to get a fair distance ahead. However, by the time they reached the tree line above the road, it was determined that the vehicle was only seconds from passing by. Thinking fast, Billy used a strategy he learned in the military called the belly crawl. With his weight dispersed over the surface of the snow, he flailed himself forward on his stomach. Sliding head-first downward, he hit the berm of the buried guardrail, which catapulted him into the air. Flipping head of heels, he landed smack dab in the middle of Devil's Slide.

"What the heck was that," Moncado blurted out from the driver's seat.

As the young man raised up out of the snow pack only twenty or so feet in front of the rescuers, McCallister announced, "That's my friend."

It was a frantic few seconds as those in the snow cat learned that the lone individual was actually not alone. As the news was shared that everyone was alive and accounted for, there was some quick rejoicing. The other six stranded soon emerged out of the tree line. Landon was surprised to see his boss, but not nearly as surprised as the Kenwoods were to see their grandpa. There were plenty of hugs and plenty of questions to be answered.

Each of the grandkids took turns hugging their grandfather. When it was Kelly's turn, her father hugged her the tightest and the longest. During their embrace he whispered in her ear, "You were always my favorite daughter."

"I'm your only daughter," she whispered back.

"Yep, the only daughter I ever wanted," he replied as their long embrace came to an end.

"Now tell me, what the hell were you all doing out in the woods?" he asked.

"We were in an old cabin across the meadow," Kelly replied.

"What cabin?"

"Mr. Cartwright's cabin!"

"Cart Chase? That crazy old Indian has been dead for over two years now".

"No Grandpa, the man with the cabin, Mr. Cartwright," Meagan chimed in.

Again, their grandfather confirmed that Cart and his wife both died when their cabin caught fire, over two years ago.

"Maybe we are talking about someone else," Kelly suggested.

Her father quickly disagreed, telling her and the others that the only cabin ever built at Unforgiven was the one Cart Chase built.

"Wait a minute, his last name was Chase, not Cartwright?" Landon asked.

"No one ever called him Cartwright. He was just known as Crazy Cart Chase."

Landon and Billy both looked at one another knowing full well what the other was thinking. There was just one more question that needed to be asked that would confirm everything. Billy inquired about Mrs. Chase, asking if she walked with a severe limp.

Though Grandpa Applegate couldn't remember, Moncado did. She had actually worked at the VA hospital where Ethlyn Chase volunteered, and confirmed that, yes, she did walk with a limp.

"She used a cane, a bright pink cane, I remember" Moncado added.

Instead of sharing what the two now knew, father and son suggested that they alone make the trek back to gather the luggage. Along the way both remained silent for a time. Billy eventually asked for his great grandmother's name.

"Ethlyn," Landon replied as he trampled forward through the snow.

As the two reached the meadow, they looked across to where the three lone pines stood. Beneath them was an old rock chimney, dusted in snow and tarnished in a black soot from a fire long ago. Had the past hours within the cabin at Unforgiven all been imagined? Was it all some kind of winter-like mirage? Landon just shook his head calling it all unbelievable. Billy, on the other hand, preferred to call it a miracle.

Off in the distance, the scraping sound of the approaching snow plows could be heard. The two turned to gather the luggage. To their surprise, the red leather-bound Bible was laying on top of the camouflage duffle bag next to a rubber-banded bundle of letters.

The sun was now above the tree line and shined directly down on the meadow. Side by side, father and son took a last look at the old rock chimney that stood strong and tall. For

Landon, it symbolized a family history, one that weathered many storms. For Billy, it was a monument to forgiveness, in a place called Unforgiven.

The End

CPSIA information can be obtained
at www.ICGtesting.com
Printed in the USA
LVHW042017080520
655247LV00003B/667

9 781631 291203